TREASURE

OF THE MAGICAL MINE MOPPETS

K.J. Blocker

Illustrated by Ron Oden

Published by Mindstir Media LLC
45 Lafayette Rd. Suite 181 | North Hampton, NH 03862 | USA
1.800.767.0531 | www.mindstirmedia.com

Printed in the United States of America
ISBN-13: 978-0-9991507-4-0
Library of Congress Control Number: 2017911094

Introduction

From a passing car in the distance, the cornfields of the farm may have looked like any other. The stalks rustled in the stiff breeze, and a green tractor kicked up dust that billowed across the landscape. A setting sun cast slim fingers of deep pinkish-red, while birds hopped from one ear to the next, as though deciding what to select for dinner.

A metallic sign read "POWERS FARM," in all caps, and under that, the phrase "Home of Ubercorn" in, ironically, small lettering. If closer to the Powers' driveway, one wouldn't need to consider what "Ubercorn" actually meant; the twenty-five-foot stalks were startling. They towered like soaring palm trees, with that same gentle sway and rhythm, calling you to come closer and rest in their shade.

A most remarkable aspect of Ubercorn was that the color gold was but a part of their endless array of hues. The top of the corn, the tassel, was the indeed golden. Yet the stalks were bolder colors—deep red, royal blue, or indigo. The leaves and silk ranged from sizzling orange to kelly green. It was a wonderland of color, painted across a forest of skyscraping corn . . .

Chapter 1

High above the earth, an old-fashioned biplane buzzed through the air, swooping down and riding the white puffy clouds.

Behind the control stick sat a man in a leather aviator helmet, the goggles covering most of his face, making him look like some sort of crop bug. He pulled on the stick with glee, and the airplane nosed even higher above the clouds.

"How's that feel, boss?" he asked Tom Powers, who had a great view of the back of the man's bulbous head from the back seat. Pressed onto Tom's head was the same sort of vintage leather aviator helmet as Tubby wore.

Tom felt less than enamored of the erratic, dizzying flight. In fact, he felt downright green but always did when flying with his field hand and pilot. "It feels real good, Tubby," Tom said, trying to sound brave and manly. "Say, how's your stomach?"

"Still there."

More than I can say, Tom thought.

Tubby pushed hard on the stick, and the nose of the plane tilted, and it dove straight down. Tom opened his mouth and screamed, but it was muffled by a white spongy cloud that smacked him square in the face. Then it popped, leaving a film of water on his cheeks.

A moment later, the plane burst out below the cloud and straightened out. Tom leaned his head over the side of the plane and peered down. Below him, on the earth, was a carpet of beautiful, rainbow-colored, towering corn stalks, swaying in the breeze, stretching nearly to the horizon. He knew those crops. They were his crops.

Ubercorn!

Hybridized, crossbred, and packed with nutrients, Ubercorn could grow three times the height of traditional corn and could be planted more densely. Tom had dedicated his life to this plant because he knew that much of the world was hungry, Ubercorn would help, and from the sale of Ubercorn he could make a good living for his wife and son. From this altitude, the vast blanket of corn looked beautiful, standing tall and thick like a giant carpet.

He watched Tubby lean on the stick again, and the plane dipped, sending Tom's stomach up to his throat.

"Which sector did you want dusted!" shouted Tubby.

"Quadrant three!" shouted Tom.

Tubby flew over the sector, flipped a gauge on his dashboard, and hit a button marked DUMP. Tom twisted around and watched as a trail of dust spewed out from behind the plane and settled down upon the crops. Tubby methodically traced rows in the sky, covering the entire quadrant.

Tom lifted a pair of binoculars to his face and watched the dissipation. He swung the binoculars across the land. Something caught his eyes, and he swung the binoculars back to see his son, Jimmy, standing and bending toward one of the cornstalks, his face nearly touching one of the huge leaves.

It was early morning, and Jimmy was making his way through the field of corn, just as he always did while waiting for the school bus to arrive. He enjoyed his walks. There was always an adventure just waiting around the bend. This morning, his daddy was taking a trip around the fields with Tubby, his pilot and farm manager. He looked up into the early morning sky to see an old beat-up crop duster flying wildly in the sky. He watched momentarily then continued down a row of corn, making his way toward the landing strip to meet his daddy when he landed.

Suddenly, something appeared in the corner of his vision. He turned to see a bug standing on the edge of one of the massive leaves. He bent over to take a look. The bug was resting just inches away from his face, and he watched spellbound as the bug lifted up its body and front legs and seemed to stare right at him. It didn't scamper off like most bugs do. Jimmy was surprised.

He examined the bug. "Whoa! You're beautiful. Where did you come from?"

He watched as the bug turned and scampered down the leaf, scaled down the stalk, reaching the bottom, and entered a small hole near the base. Moments later it reappeared and looked up at Jimmy as if it understood his very words and was answering his question. It assumed an almost human stance as it lifted one of its front legs and seemed to salute.

Jimmy was awestruck by the behavior and started to reach out to touch the magnificent specimen when he heard a buzzing sound coming from the sky nearby. He looked up to see his daddy's crop duster flying toward the landing strip. He looked at the bug once more, telling, first himself, and then the bug, "I've got to go now. I will return as soon as I get home from school."

He lifted up and began running down the row of corn to meet his daddy and tell him of his discovery.

As the crop duster circled about, Tom watched the tiny figure, Jimmy, through the binoculars, curious why he was so interested in a leaf and what exactly had caught his attention so intently. Just as the plane was about to turn close to the landing strip, he saw Jimmy leap up and run across the dirt strip.

"All right," shouted Tom above the racket of the old motor, "you can put her down now. Watch out for Jimmy!"

Tubby wheeled the plane around and headed toward the short landing strip. It was tucked in alongside a warren of houses in the middle of the rainbow-colored property. From here, Tom could see the single dirt lane that connected the compound with the main road.

The plane touched down with a jolt and a screech and then rumbled and clattered to a halt. Tubby turned off the engine. Tom hoisted himself out of his seat, jumped over the edge of the plane, and landed on the hard-packed ground. He stretched, then heard a shout.

"Daddy!"

Tom spun around. Nine-year-old Jimmy was sprinting across the ground toward him, his shaggy brown hair bouncing, and bright, big, brown eyes shining in the sunlight. In one hand was a kite as colorful as the Ubercorn, and in the other hand was the spool. He kept tripping over the string which dangled between the kite and the spool, but he never lost his balance.

"Hey there!" Tom shouted.

The boy slid to a stop and affixed himself to his daddy's leg. "I saw you! You were flying crazy!"

"That's what happens when Tubby takes the stick!" he said. "Look at him. Doesn't he look like a crazy pilot?"

Tubby, rubbing down the exterior skin of the plane, made a wild face at the boy. Jimmy giggled, and Tom gently detached his son from his leg. Then he took the kite from his son's hand and looked at it. "I bet you want some help learning how to fly that kite," he said.

"Yeah! But it's all tangled up!"

"We'll untangle it and fly it soon, but not today." His son looked crestfallen. "We will, Jimmy!"

Jimmy stamped his foot. "You promised we would do it today! Remember?"

Tom scratched his head. He felt bad about it, but he had to face Mr. Withers, as much as he hated to. "I've spent a little too much time in the air already, and I have an important meeting today." He tousled his son's hair. "We'll do it tomorrow."

Then he pulled his briefcase out of the back seat of the plane and headed for the car, shouting over his shoulder. "Ask Tubby for help! Sorry! Next time, though!"

Chapter 2

Tom shaded his eyes with his hand and stared up the endless flight of steps, wondering just how long it would take him to climb up.

He stood at the foot of the Mighty Bank of Elites. This massive temple to money and the almighty interest rate looked like a Greek temple, designed to make all entrants feel as though they were puny, insignificant, lower than a snake's belly. It towered over Tom both physically and financially, making him certainly *feel* insignificant.

He had come here to beg forgiveness for his farm loan, and that alone made him feel sort of like a failure and nobody.

Sighing, Tom dragged himself up the long staircase and into the open maw of the front door, completely out of breath. A thin, prissy man sat behind a desk, a self-satisfied look on his face. A headset rested comfortably on the left side of his head.

"May I help you?" he said robotically.

"I have an appointment to meet Mr. Withers," said Tom.

The man's face grew serious. "Your name?"

"Tom Powers."

He looked on his screen. "It's at twelve p.m., correct?"

"It is."

He stood up. "Right this way, sir."

He followed the man through the labyrinth of hallways, up another set of stairs, and finally to the top floor. He glanced out a window, and the height here made him feel a little queasy like he was back up in the crop dusting plane with Tubby.

The entire top floor was wide open, and a battalion of four other receptionists, all women, lined the walls. At the far end of the room was a single intimidating door.

It read, in large, bold letters, "MR. WITHERS. BANK PRESIDENT."

Tom gulped and straightened his tie.

"You can go right in," said the man who'd accompanied him. "Just check in with her first."

He pointed to the first of the four receptionists. Tom walked over to her desk and introduced himself. The first receptionist checked her log book. "Ah, yes, I see—you'll have to head over and check in with her." She pointed to another receptionist.

Tom walked over to the second receptionist. She pointed to a nearby chair and said nothing.

Tom took a seat and crossed his legs and twiddled his thumbs and was consumed with memories of being summoned to the principal's office.

"You'll have to fill out this form," another woman, from behind him said, handing him a clipboard. Tom looked at the form. It asked for a long list of personal and financial details. He sighed, filled it in, and handed it back to her. The third receptionist refused to take it. "You have to give it to her," she said, pointing to a fourth receptionist.

Tom dutifully headed over to the fourth woman. She was analyzing a chart of numbers. "Would you like this form?" he said.

She looked up over her spectacles, taking in Tom's earnest face, then going down to the clipboard. She took it away from him and read over the lines.

"There's a problem," she said. "You forgot to check the box marked gender."

"Let me guess," he replied. "I can only make corrections by going back to the first receptionist."

"Heavens no, that would be inefficient. I'll correct it for you."

She used her pencil to scratch out a single letter. Then she said, "Go ahead, over to Mr. Withers's door."

Tom shuffled over to the door and lifted his hand to knock on it as commanded. His heart was hammering against the inside of his chest.

The third receptionist stood up. "I'm sorry, you can't do that. Only I can knock on the door."

Tom stepped aside as she came over and knocked on the door. Then she returned to her seat.

"Enter," shouted a muffled voice from the other side.

Tom took a deep breath and pushed inside.

It was an excruciatingly simple office. The walls were brown paneling, and the carpet was stained by years of wear. Tom immediately felt stifled in the thick air and wished that someone would open a window. Behind an old-school mahogany desk that looked like it had been bought more than forty years ago sat a man.

Mr. Withers.

He was dressed in a striped gray suit that was a little too large for him. His short hair was graying, his hands thin and pale, his Adam's apple prominent. A half-eaten submarine sandwich sat on the desk next to him. When he saw Tom enter, he immediately wrapped it up, sealing the paper with a piece of cellophane tape, then shoved it into a desk drawer.

"Yes," he said, "you surprised me. I didn't know you would enter so fast."

"You told me to enter, Mr. Withers."

"So I did," he said, "so I did."

The bank president stood up and shook hands with Tom. Then he wiped his hand on his pants, a faint signal of disgust passing across his face.

They both sat down, Tom occupying the hot seat directly in front of the desk. He figured that many pleas had been heard in this chair.

"How is the family?" asked Withers.

"My wife is fine," replied Tom, "and my son too. Have you met them?"

"No," replied the bank president, flatly, "but it's something I ask everybody because I'm supposed to pretend that I care about other people's lives."

Tom didn't know what to say to that, so he finally chimed in with, "Well, that's honest and forthright of you. Let's get down to business."

"Yes," said Withers, making a show of pulling a file out of his desk and placing it squarely before him on the desk. His hands straightened the manila folder, compulsively, until it was perpendicular to the edge of the desk.

"I'm here because I've missed a loan payment."

"You've missed two."

Tom nodded, bowing his head. If he'd worn a hat, he'd have put it between his hands.

"According to the rules of the loan, you have a third payment due in three weeks."

"I do."

"And if you don't make this payment, you will default on the loan, and this bank will repossess your farm." Withers's hands compulsively straightened the file folder again.

Tom fought the urge to sweep the file folder off the desk. "I have good news. Number one, we have a huge crop coming in this year, really good, one of the best ever. And number two, I have a bevy of investors who are about to write me big checks to own a chunk of my burgeoning Ubercorn empire. I'll easily be able to repay those missed payments."

"We'll see."

Withers just folded his hands and looked at him like a man stares at an annoying bug that's flitting around just out of reach. Tom grew more anxious. "Look, Mr. Withers, I just need more time. Ubercorn is going to be worth billions. No doubt, I'm onto something here."

MIGHTY BANK OF ELITES

"Perhaps, Mr. Powers," replied the bank president, "but right now it's worth pennies. You have three weeks, Tom. Twenty-one days until your next payment or the farm is mine. The bank's, I mean."

He put the file folder into his desk and snapped to his feet. Tom realized that the meeting was over. He stood up as well and offered his hand. A disgusted crinkle of a smile came across Withers's face as they shook hands. He wiped it off on his pants as Tom turned.

Withers watched as Tom left the office. When the door had closed behind him, Withers went over to the closet and opened the door. A young Asian man in a suit practically fell out of the closet. Gasping for breath, he started waving a sheaf of papers.

"You'll get your own office soon enough, Young Lin," said Withers, "with ventilation and everything."

"I'm responsible, Mr. Withers. You can trust me. I'd like a desk someday."

"At this bank, you have to earn a desk. You've only been here two years."

The president sat down behind his desk, removed the submarine sandwich from the desk drawer, carefully unwrapped it, and took a bite. He sat there, chewing, as the young man stayed standing.

"May I leave, sir?" asked Young Lin.

Swallowing, Withers ignored the question. "Tom Powers is going to go bankrupt on a hybridized crop that could save the world. When I repossess that farm, I'm going to make billions."

"Yes sir," said Young Lin, making notes in his notebook. "Repossess farm, make billions."

Withers put down his sandwich, as though he'd been struck by a great insight. "Do you know who Tom's father is?"

"I have no idea, sir."

"Of course you don't. You're young and stupid."

Withers stood up and looked out the tiny frosted window, his back to his assistant. "Pappy, his name is Pappy."

Young Lin wrote down the name. "P-a-p-p-y. That's his real name?"

"That's all anyone has ever called him for, well, forever. Long story. So, this Pappy has a salt mine—and he owes me."

The assistant ventured a question. "Is he behind on his payments too?"

"No, it's nothing financial. It's older, much older, much more personal. He owes me something else." Withers looked out the window for a moment, deep in thought. "I want his salt mine."

Young Lin stood there, not knowing what to do. "But . . . salt? Salt is about worthless, isn't it? I mean, it's not exactly gold."

Withers slammed his fist on the desk. Young Lin was supposed to be smart, but he sure could act the idiot at times. "This salt is better than gold! It's Pappy's."

Withers turned toward Young Lin. He pointed to his assistant's notepad. Young Lin finally got a clue and scribbled away, saying aloud, "Take-Pappy's-mine."

When he'd finished, Withers waved him off. "Leave us." Withers loved the royal "us."

"Yes sir," said Young Lin, hustling out of the room, glad not to go back in that closet.

Withers leaned back in his upholstered leather chair. He felt good, yes he did. Now he had some scheming to do, and he got to it.

Chapter 3

That night, Tom sat up late in his recliner, a large photo album on his lap. His wife, Mary Anne, padded into the room. She was a farm gal, smart, strong, and a good mother. She was the type of woman that you make a life with.

Seeing her, he snatched a nearby sheaf of Ubercorn stats and tossed it on top of the album. "I was just looking at the P & Ls," he said, "and I think we're gonna make it. Barely, but it's doable."

Mary Anne walked over to the recliner. Without a word, she reached down and picked up the sheaf of statistics. She glanced at the photo album. "What are you looking at?"

He looked down. The album was open to the photo of a six-year-old Tom next to a young man dressed in dusty dungarees. There was a determined light in the young man's eyes as he looked directly into the camera. He seemed unaware of the boy next to him.

"Pappy," he said.

Mary Anne looked longingly at the photo. "It's too bad Jimmy won't ever get to know him."

"I barely knew him," said Tom. His wife kissed him on the top of his head. "Don't stay up too late."

"I won't. I'm getting tired."

She left the room, and Tom looked down at the photo again. He felt himself tunnel backward in time . . .

. . . all the way to age six, to the moment when he had watched his father enter the house, his eyes shining, and shouting. "Boy, I've got news fer ya—I've found it!"

Tom, wearing his baseball uniform, barreled over, and affixed himself to his father's leg. "You were gone two weeks, Daddy!"

His father had detached him gently from his leg and tousled his head. "Don't worry 'bout that. Just listen ta what I have ta say. I bought a mine, a real mine, and it's packed full a treasure. Real treasure, the likes a which the world has never seen." He'd crouched down and looked into the young boy's eyes. "We're gonna be rich, son."

Tom had searched his father's eyes. "When can we play ball?"

"Soon," said his father, standing up, "I promise. Right now, I got work ta do, but soon!"

Tom watched him stomp off through the house, calling for Tom's mother.

He'd left that night for two months. By the time he was eighteen, Tom felt as *though he had barely ever spent time with Pappy.*

In his recliner, Tom focused on the photo again and snapped out of his memories. He closed the photo album and put it on a shelf and hiked upstairs to bed.

Chapter 4

At breakfast the next morning, Tom sat chewing his bacon morosely. On the other side of the long farmhouse table, Jimmy had finished off his plate and was racing a toy car across the edge of the table. He was running it left, right, flying it through the air, making explosion sounds.

Then he accidentally dropped it onto a plate. The sound of metal hitting ceramic jarred Tom out of his thoughts."

Aren't you getting a little too old to be playing with toy cars, boy?" he snapped. He snatched the car away.

Jimmy looked at his daddy with solemn eyes and hung his head.

At the fridge, Mary Anne said, "Tom? Jimmy has something he wants to tell you."

Tom heard her, but her words didn't quite sink in. His eyes were fixed on a corner of the room while his untouched coffee gradually cooled in its mug. He propped his elbow on the table and plopped his forehead into his palm, hoping he had come up with an answer to their financial plight. "So here's my calculation. If we could find a source of cash to float us for one month, it would give me time to get the commitment from those investors."

"Your son wants to—"

He continued, lest he lose his line of thinking. "That source could come from anywhere. I mean, banks make small business loans all the time to help entrepreneurs stay afloat. And Withers didn't even offer that yesterday. Of course not. I think he wants me to fail. He knows that this is going to make everybody who touches it a billionaire, and he figures if the bank can get control over it—well, that's the end game. Someday we're going to look back on these days and shake our heads and laugh—"

"Tom!" Mary Anne exclaimed.

He had to pay attention, now. "What?"

She drew close to him and bent down, almost whispering. "Your son has something to tell you."

Tom looked over at Jimmy. "He wants to tell me something?"

She laid a kindly hand on her son's shoulders. "Go on, Jimmy. Tell your daddy what happened at school yesterday."

The boy looked down at his hands, his legs dangling in the adult chair. He said something in a small voice.

Tom leaned forward. "Speak up, son. What are you trying to say? Did someone beat you up?"

His son reluctantly spoke louder. "I said I won a science competition."

"You won a science competition? There was a science competition?"

"Yes," said Mary Anne, "and he took first place. You were too busy yesterday to hear the news."

Tom sat back in his chair. "Wow, that's really something else."

"Tell your daddy about the project."

Jimmy was still remarkably quiet, unable to meet his daddy's eyes, oddly bashful for his success. "It was a project . . . about a house in the desert . . . and you could save water by tilting the roof so that it runs down the roof into a . . . what's it called?"

"A cistern," said Mary Anne.

"A cistern," he repeated, "and then you store the water underground so that the hot weather doesn't make it evaporate."

Tom was impressed. His son had been evidently listening to all the conversations he'd been having over the last few years about irrigation. "So you drew it out?"

Jimmy nodded. "I put it on paper, and then I put the paper on a big blue board with glue."

Tom turned to his wife. "You helped him with this?"

"I just bought the board and the paper. The rest was all him."

"Well done," said Tom. "See, he didn't need my help."

"The judging took place yesterday afternoon," said Mary Anne. "All the parents were there. You should have been, don't you think?"

Tom took a sip of coffee. Then he set the mug down with more force than he had intended. "Well, I guess I should apologize for creating a hybridized strain of corn that's going to feed starving people everywhere! I'm sorry for trying to change the world!"

His son was looking at him with fear. His wife tried to soothe him. "Nobody's trying to—"

"Maybe I should've just settled for an ordinary life! Maybe I should've just become a cubicle slave! Then I could be home at six p.m. every night, no worries, steady paycheck. I'd be there for every one of Jimmy's band concerts and soccer games and science competitions."

"I play baseball, Daddy!" Jimmy shouted.

"Jimmy, go run and play," said Mary Anne, "while I talk to your daddy alone."

His son jumped down off his chair and walked around the table, careful to avoid his daddy. Then he picked up his toy car and put it in his pocket, cast a sideways glance at Tom, and left the room. The screen door slammed behind him.

Mary put her hands on her hips and stared icily at him, and he knew he had been wrong.

"Sorry," Tom said. "I'll go tell him I'm sorry." He got to his feet and headed for the door. "I'm letting stress get to me."

Chapter 5

That afternoon, Mary Anne stood in the doorway of the granary, watching the hired help push around the corn.

Storing corn wasn't as easy as it sounded, and Ubercorn had some particular challenges. Mary Anne didn't have any expertise in chemistry or agriculture, but she had found this niche in the system—the granary. She could be counted on to build and follow a schedule.

She pointed to a vat marked Schedule 4. "That one needs a touch of water, guys."

One of them gave her a thumbs-up. That was enough for her. She trusted the workers' expertise and left the barn. She crossed the hot dirt toward the headquarters, a two-story ranch-style building. She entered her office, which was adjacent to her husband's, and sat down at her desk. She had just logged in to her computer when the office telephone rang.

It wasn't the normal ring tone volume. It was muted. Her eyes flicked down. It was the home line that was ringing. They'd connected the home line to the office two years ago so that Tom could talk to his family without walking back to the house, and so any calls to home from outside callers could be received if they were busy at the office.

She picked up the receiver and hit the line. "Hello?"

A strange old man's voice said, "Mary Anne?"

"Yes?"

"It's Pappy."

She didn't say anything, feeling struck dumb. "I don't understand. Pappy who?"

"Tom's dad."

"I'm sorry, Tom's father is dead."

"I see reports of my demise have been greatly exaggerated, as Mr. Clements said. I want ta talk ta my son."

Still dumbfounded, Mary Anne found herself grabbing a pen and a pink memo pad—the type that read While you were out—and resorting to secretary speak. "I'm sorry, he's in a meeting. Can I take a message?"

"Yes, tell 'im ta call me." The strange voice told her a phone number.

She dutifully wrote it down. "I'll give it to him as soon as I see him."

"Thank ya kindly," he responded.

He disconnected. She sat there and looked at the phone, then at the message pad. Something very strange was going on here.

At dinner that night, Tom was on another roll. It had been a nonstop monologue, full of more wild ideas for making the next payment on the loan. He gesticulated with his fork, waving it around in the air like a conductor waving his baton.

Mary Anne listened to all of it. She knew the importance of supporting her husband whenever possible. This was one of those times. However, she was also waiting for an opportunity to break in.

He paused to chew a piece of meat. She saw her chance. "Honey," she said.

His mouth full, he retorted, "Sorry, hang on, I'm trying to think!"

Mary Anne reached over and touched her son's arm. "Your daddy thinks by talking out loud."

"It's true," Tom nodded, finally swallowing.

With a lull in the monologue, Mary Anne saw her opportunity. "A strange person called for you today, honey."

"Who was that?"

"He said he was your dad."

Tom stopped chewing. He stared at her as though she had grown three heads.

Mary Anne took another bite of her dinner, then said, "But I knew that wasn't possible."

Tom was indignant. "What kind of sick joker would say such a thing? Making fun of a family tragedy."

"You mean the squirrel?" Jimmy asked. Her son looked quite concerned. "How he got stuck inside the machine?"

"That's right," said Tom. "My father, your grandfather, stuck his arm into a threshing machine to rescue a trapped squirrel. It killed him. I was out of state, and nobody could reach me. I didn't hear about it until a week later. I missed the funeral."

"Well, if you want to chew the guy out, here's the number." Mary Anne held up the pink memo with the number. She passed it across the table to Tom. He barely glanced at it.

She shrugged. "This guy said Mr. Clements seemed to think his death was exaggerated."

"That's absurd," Tom scoffed. "Who is Mr. Clements?

"I don't know. I thought you might. He sounded sincere."

He shoved the pink memo back toward his wife. "You know what, I'm not even going to bother calling this fool. He should've had more respect for the dead."

Mary Anne stood up and left the table with Pappy's number in her hand. She placed her plate in the sink and put the pink memo into the trash can.

Later that night, when the house was quiet, a dark figure sneaked stealthily down the hallway. His feet carefully dodged the creaky spots on the hardwood floors. He tried not to breathe until he reached the kitchen, where he leaned against the counter, proud of making it there undetected.

He lifted the lid of the trash can and rummaged through it. "Come on. I know you're in here, Pappy. Ah-ha—there."

He lifted up the crumpled scrap of pink paper. He carefully folded it and stuffed it in his pocket and sneaked out of the kitchen.

Early the next morning, Jimmy knocked on the master bathroom door, "Daddy? Are you in there?"

"I'll be out in a second son," Tom said. He was sitting on the side of the bathtub with his phone in one hand and the crumpled sheet of paper in the other. He turned on the faucet to drown out the sound of what he was about to do.

"But I need to brush my teeth before school!"

He cupped his hand around his mouth and raised his voice. "Everyone needs a break from hygiene once in a while, son. Today's your day. Congratulations on the science competition!"

Tom heard his son's footsteps fade down the hall. He quickly dialed and pressed the phone tightly to his ear.

After only two rings, a once-familiar voice answered. "Hello?"

Son of a gun, Tom thought and managed to squeak out the words, "I'm looking for a, um, Pappy?"

"Ya got 'im."

"My name is Tom Powers," he said.

"I know that. I chose it, Thomas Cole Powers" the voice said, matter-of-factly.

"Is it really you, Pappy?"

"Yep."

Tom felt the blood rise into his neck and up to his cheeks. "Why did you

32

call me? After all these years?"

"I'd like ta come visit ya," Pappy said. His answers were quick like he'd already considered all the ways this conversation might come together.

"You can't," Tom said.

Pappy's voice didn't waiver. "I have ta talk ta ya. It's important."

Banging on the door made Tom jump practically to the ceiling. The phone flew out of his hands, but he was lucky enough to catch it.

"Tom?" Mary Anne said. "Jimmy needs to brush his teeth. The faucet in his bathroom broke."

"One minute, sweetie." Tom cupped the phone and spoke in an angry whisper. "Pappy, my family thinks you're dead!"

"Well, whose fault is that?"

The banging on the door grew louder. Tom thought quickly. "Well, yours. At least mostly. I didn't want to explain to them what a lousy dad you were. I really did it to save you."

Pappy and Tom were both silent a moment.

Then Tom spoke up. "Meet me tomorrow morning at Madge's Diner. You remember where that is?"

"Of course. I'm old, not dead. That Madge loves me."

"Right."

"Don't ferget ta show up, Tom."

"I should be saying that to you, Pappy."

He ended the call, then turned off the water faucet. He flung open the door to find Mary Anne standing there, hand on a hip, their son next to her looking at him with baleful eyes.

"Who were you talking to?"

"No one, I was just . . . trying to meditate. And I had another great idea. Listen to this."

He threw his arm over his wife's shoulder.

Chapter 6

Tom had wrapped his hands around his coffee mug so tightly that he was starting to scald his fingers.

He was sitting in a booth at Madge's Diner. It was a throwback diner, the kind of place where the seats were vinyl, and country-fried steak had been on the menu for at least eighty years and was still a Thursday special. The waitresses wore too much makeup, were full of smiles, and dispensed top-offs of coffee with acute awareness. A sign in the corner read Welcome to Madge's. Every plate served with a side of local gossip!

That was doubly true for the owner, Madge. She was what is colloquially known as a piece of work. Shorter than a Maya, wide as a wheelbarrow, she wore her orange hair piled in a side knot, and her lipstick was red, always very, very red. She moved from table to table with the stainless steel coffee pot. But her looks could be deceiving—she had given the diner a reputation for being the hub of all town goings-on. Part of that was due to the fifteen hours a day that she put in here. Part of it was also due to her astuteness. Her ear was keener than a hound dog's, and she sized you up the moment you walked in the door.

Tom checked his watch. He had arrived half an hour ago, and Pappy still hadn't shown up.

"You're gonna break my mug, you squeeze it any tighter." It was Madge. She topped him off.

"I'm waiting for my father," he replied.

"Your father?"

"I haven't seen him in years."

Her eyebrow went up. "You talkin' about Pappy?" The one who ran off to the mine all those years ago?"

"Yeah."

Madge paused. "Well, knock me over with a feather. He must've got lost down there then found his way out. I asked around of his whereabouts but got nothin'. He never showed up again. He just disappeared. Don't know how he could've survived all these years, but I guess miracles do still happen."

Tom shook his head. She cocked her head, thinking, then shook it off and grinned. "Glad he survived. Can't wait to see him!"

She moved along, and Tom amused himself for the next couple of minutes by pulverizing a packet of crackers inside its plastic wrapper. Then the door to the diner opened.

It was Pappy. He had changed some, aged quite a bit. But it was Pappy.

As Pappy stepped through the doorway of the diner, Tom got to his feet and sized up the man he knew to be his father. He sported long, gnarly hair parted down the middle and plain, rugged clothing. His eyes were gray, gleaming with wildness.

"Pappy?" Tom asked.

"It's me, in the flesh!" Pappy smiled, which made Tom suddenly angry. He knew that his own moods were whipsawing, but he could not wrap his head around what the old man had done. Barely seeing him for all those years, and now, suddenly, dropping by like an old pal.

Tom put his hands on his hips. "I don't know whether to hug you or punch you.

"Pappy shrugged. "I would punch me."

Instinctively, Tom's right hand balled into a fist and rose up, cocked and ready, but then he gathered his wits and lowered his arm. "I can't punch my own father."

Pappy shook his head, "Still indecisive," he said. "How 'bout we just shake hands?"

Tom tried to relax and stuck his hand out. Pappy shook it. The old man's hand felt calloused and old but still strong.

They took a seat in the booth. Madge came over with a coffee mug and stood over Pappy, beaming. "Good afternoon, Pappy. Remember me?"

"I sure do!"

She wiggled a bit, then reached down and pinched Pappy's cheek. "You are still adorable!"

Wow, thought Tom. Madge has a thing for Pappy after all these years!

"Y'all want somethin' for breakfast?" she asked.

Tom looked at his father. "Are you hungry?"

"Ya could bring me three strips a bacon and a side a pickles."

Madge paused for a moment. "Same old Pappy, same old breakfast order! Tom?"

"Coffee's fine."

She walked off, and the awkwardness descended between father and son like a red curtain.

Tom finally said, "So why did you call? What do you want?"

Pappy's eyes were bright and focused. "We need your help, son. We have big problems!"

"Who is we?"

"You and me."

Tom held up a hand. "Wait, wait. We're not a team, Pappy. I haven't even heard from you in years. I told people you were dead."

His father scratched his head. "So I heard. It came to that, did it?"

"Yes, it did."

Then Pappy's mind seemed to spin off to something else. "But I tell you, the banker—he's trouble, big trouble! We need your help, or I lose the mine!"

"Who's we?" Tom asked. "It's certainly not you and me."

"Me and Mr. Clements."

"Why not just get Mr. Clements help."

"Cain't. He's not here."

"Well, where is he?" Tom asked.

"Somewheres. I don't know. Maybe at the mine or he could be here right now."

"Do you see him?"

"Well no, but that don't mean he ain't here. I need ta know if you're willin' ta help us save my mine."

Tom hadn't seen him in so long that there had been no telling what Pappy was like today, or if he'd maintained all his faculties, or what few he ever had. Truth was, he sounded a lot like a looney old man. Pappy hadn't exactly been lucid all those years ago, either.

"It's a salt mine, right?"

"Yes, and they're comin' after it!"

"Who's coming after it?"

"The bank, I told ya," said Pappy. "They're gonna repossess it."

The weight of the irony nearly crushed Tom. "You're not the only one with the bank on his heels."

"Oh yeah? Who else?"

"Me. My farm . . . it's not doing well."

His father looked puzzled. "Ya have a farm?"

Tom buried his head in his arms on the table. His father didn't even know what he did for a living, didn't have a clue how he'd dedicated his life to making Ubercorn happen. He didn't even know he had kept the family farm.

Finally, Tom lifted his head. "Yes, with thousands of acres and a cutting-edge crop. But that's not important. What's important is us, our relationship. You come here asking for help, but what have you ever done for me, except leave? All my life you went away for a week here, then a month there, then half a year. After Mom died, you just took off permanently."

"You was eighteen, ya weren't a child," his father mumbled.

A hysterical note appeared in Tom's voice, and he forced it back down. "I could've talked to you! I could've used . . . someone! But you were gone!"

"I was granted special access ta the mine," said Pappy, "and believe me, it wasn't easy ta get. Them Magical Mine Moppets don't open their doors fer just anybody."

Tom made a pfft sound. "The Magical Mine Moppets." Again Pappy was ranting about these so-called Magical Mine Moppets, some fantasy creatures that Pappy had conjured up in one of his wild episodes.

Pappy ignored the jibe. "I need ta know if you're willin' ta help me save my mine."

Tom looked at him dead in the eye. "I have my own problems. And if you'll excuse me, I've got to get back to saving 'my' farm."

Madge came over with the plate of bacon and side of pickles and placed it in front of him. "Sorry for the wait, but I had to repeat the order to the cook twice. He'd never heard of that before. He's new. Only been here ten years or so."

Pappy said nothing.

She stared at him, feeling pity. "You guys having a tough time together?"

Pappy sighed. "Yep."

Tom stood up, offered his hand. Pappy shook it weakly, then dropped his head. Tom dropped some money on the table and walked out of the diner.

Chapter 7

The next morning, Tom was the first one up and moving around the house. An internal alarm popped his eyes open no later than five a.m. After so many years of resisting it, he had simply embraced it. He was an early riser, like it or not.

Tom hustled outside, stomped up to the door of Tubby's apartment and office, and banged on it. Tubby answered, blinking away the sunlight. A cluster of hair stuck up to the sky, and he scratched his big belly.

"Rise and shine, Tubby!" Tom said, blowing past him.

Tubby rubbed his eyes and shut the door behind Tom. "I was up late prayin' for help." Tubby accidentally kicked an empty bottle when he walked back to his desk. It clinked against the nearest wall.

"I'm sure you were. So today is the day."

"What day?"

"The day that we're going to solve all our problems. Investor day!"

"We'll be lucky to be in business this time next year," Tubby said.

"I'm gonna pretend you didn't just say that."

"Hey, Tom! Guess who's here?"

"Who?"

He pointed to the doorway. "Your favorite little kite flyer!"

Little Jimmy was standing in the doorway of the office. "Hi, Daddy."

He rounded the corner of the desk and crouched down before his son. The boy was wearing pajamas and muddy sneakers. "What're you doing out here so early?"

"I was in the field. Look!"

His son pulled away from him and opened his palm. Inside was a squat insect, with ten legs, a pair of wiggling antenna, and a pair of bright rainbow-colored wings. It crawled around as Jimmy kept his hand rotating to maintain control over the little critter.

"What is that?" Tom asked aloud.

"Her name is Lacey," said Jimmy. "She told me so. She wrote it in the dirt."

Tom thought about that. Jimmy had a vivid imagination, but then he was still young. He remembered how he used to pretend with his toys and play with different things creating stories. That was until his father started coming home talking about these magical mine creatures. At first, he had believed him, but over time, as his father's visits home became less frequent, he started realizing that imaginary thoughts could bring nothing but pain.

"That's nice, Jimmy," Tom replied. Now was not the time to have a discussion about how he felt about imaginary friends. He concentrated instead upon the little funny looking caterpillar shaped bug with the face and eyes of a beetle and wings upon its back.

Tubby crowded over them. "It's plump and shiny like an ant, but with the fierce stance and surly countenance of a bumblebee."

Tom looked up at him. "That was very poetic, Tubby."

The pilot shrugged, a dull, puzzled look crossing his face. "Yeah, I don't know where it comes from."

Tom sat back on his heels, looking at the thing. In past years, he had carefully placed rubber bands and clothespins in various places on the ear to keep the corn safe, and once helped Jimmy draw eyeballs on a mangy-looking scarecrow they had rigged together. He was always thinking of ways to protect the corn and nurture it to grow even taller than it already was.

Jimmy's morning discovery, however, seemed an entirely new addition to the Ubercorn fields. Tom didn't like it. The sight of this heretofore-unseen critter was, he figured, a bad omen. Maybe this was why a section of his crop was looking a little sickly. He'd have to investigate.

"I found her in the field," said Jimmy.

Tom gazed at it. "I've never seen anything like it." Tubby snapped his fingers. "You know, I think it kinda looks like a Skeletonizer Bug."

"You've seen one before?" said Tom.

"Yeah. This one looks like the youth stage with the caterpillar body and wings. It will soon lose the legs and have a long thin body. You know, they like to eat soybeans."

"We're not growing soybeans," said Tom.

"I think she's trying to say something," said Jimmy. The bug was standing in his hand, waving its feelers erratically.

"I doubt it," said Tom. "Bugs can't talk." He turned to the computer, opened the browser, and typed in Skeletonizer Bug. He spent a minute reading in silence, trying to figure out what this weird bug was and learn if it posed a threat to the Ubercorn. It didn't look as if it did.

He sat back, looked over at his son. "It doesn't eat corn, only soybeans, like Tubby said. And willow trees, they have some strange compound that it likes."

"Can I keep this one?" said Jimmy, admiring the bug.

"Just toss it back in the fields. It belongs in nature."

"Hey, she just winked at me! I really think she's trying to tell me something. She's moving her front legs up. They're moving about like little hands playing charades."

Tom tried not to smile. "I'm sure that's just some natural bug dance movement. Now, run along and get breakfast," he gently commanded.

The boy scooted out the door.

"Don't say goodbye to me," said Tubby, with mock anger.

"Bye, Tubby!" came Jimmy's voice from the path. "I'm gonna put the Skeletonizer back!"

"Don't forget your ballgame today!" Tubby, yelled.

"Ballgame?" Tom asked. He had forgotten the boy's game again. He hoped his farm tour was successful and efficiently quick. He couldn't miss another of Jimmy's events.

Tom looked out the window and watched Jimmy trot into the fields.

Jimmy ran as fast as his little legs could go to his secret spot near the house where he gently put his new friend down on a nice leaf bed near the bottom of one of the towering corn stalks. He had made the bed just for Lacey then had gone to find her where he had found her and then left her a few days ago.

Lacey looked up at Jimmy and laid her belly on the bed and curled up content.

Jimmy watched her and then said, "I have to go to school now. I know you don't know what that is, but don't worry, I'll be back soon." He took his finger and gently stroked her closed wings. Then he jumped up and ran toward the house.

Chapter 8

Tom felt his strides growing longer, his voice growing stronger, as he led the group of international visitors through the farm offices.

It was three o'clock, and the group of Japanese investors had been asking him a series of very pointed questions for the last two hours. He had done his best to answer them, but the questions just kept on coming, and he was feeling more anxious. Tom didn't want to let on just how much was on the line, but without an outside injection of cash, there was no doubt that the future of Ubercorn would be counted not in years, but in days.

"Ubercorn can nearly double the supply of corn in just five years," he said, doing his best to smile like a beauty queen. "Think of how we can reduce worldwide hunger! We are the first to develop this world-changing corn, the first to grow it, and will be the first to market it."

One of the Japanese whispered to the translator. The translator raised his hand. "And what is the current debt incurred by the company?"

Tom gulped, then scrambled for an answer. "All companies carry debt, sir. You know what we say around here? You're not a company if you're not up to your ears in debt." He pointed in the direction of the fields. "Ears of corn, that is!"

The translator grimaced. Tom waved it off.

He led them into a hallway, where slickly produced industrial videos of Ubercorn played on screens that lined the walls. Construction workers were at the far end of the hallway on ladders and scaffolds covering a mural with a long rainbow-colored curtain. Behind it, the mural portrayed a depiction of poor, hungry, yet smiling, women and children being handed rainbow-colored corn meal in flour sacks.

Suddenly, Jimmy rushed in from the far end of the hallway, nearly knocking over the workers. He sprinted up to his father, looking like a Norman Rockwell all-American kid, dragging a tangled kite behind him.

"Hey, Daddy!" he called out. "Can you help me fix my kite now?"

"It's my son, Jimmy," Tom whispered to the group. Turning to his son, he said firmly, "You'll have to wait outside until I'm finished with this meeting."

"But Daddy—"

Under his breath, Tom added, "Not now, these are important people. Go outside!"

Turning his back on his son, he faced the group of potential Ubercorn investors. "Now, let's see what the future holds for Ubercorn!"

The circle of people closed around Tom again, and they shuffled forward, passing around the forlorn little boy, his kite drooping on the floor. Tom felt bad, but this simply was not the time.

They moved as a unit down the hall, a panoramic window with a black shade pulled tight over the glass on one side, and more video screens on the other. The workers were just putting away the last of their equipment when Tom stopped the group safely close to the covered mural. "After two hours, I bet you're wondering something. You're wondering, Mr. Powers, wouldn't it be great if we could experience what it's like to see the faces of the world when they are fed and have plentiful supply? Now that moment has arrived."

He reached out to a control panel on the wall and stabbed it with a flamboyant show of force.

"Ubercorn Revolution!" he shouted.

Unexpectedly, the black shade snapped up, and sunlight poured into the room. Tom watched the faces of the Japanese investors. They looked shocked, which was typical. But instead of registering delight and joy, their faces turned into horrified grimaces. One man let out a gasp of horror. Tom swung around, confused by the responses, and froze, staring at the horrific scene in front of him. The open window displayed the vista of Ubercorn.

It was dead.

Row after row were desiccated, the color of chalk. His skin suddenly felt superheated as he tugged at his collar like a bad comedian. What happened?

He stammered an excuse. "So, uh, if you keep watching the video screens behind you, behind you, you'll see even more vibrant colors and the delicious freshness of our product."

He frantically jabbed the button on the control. Nothing happened. He stepped forward and manually yanked down the shade, which broke loose and tumbled and clanked to the ground in a tangled mess.

From his back pocket, Tom pulled a two-way radio and hit the talk button. "Hey, this is an APB. Tank, please grab your crew and more curtains and come cover the display window. Urgent."

Within a minute, a pair of the workers wearing bright red Ubercorn shirts appeared in the hall. They began nailing curtains up over the glass. "Just a little construction here," Tom explained lamely. "We're always improving ourselves here at Ubercorn."

One of the businessmen, a scowl on his face, finally spoke up. "Mr. Powers, your corn does not look healthy."

Tom grasped for an excuse. "You know, we've had an irrigation problem. Of course, we caught it. We'll get 'er straightened out."

Jimmy shouldered his way through the group and tugged at Tom's arm. "Daddy, it's important. I really got to show you something. I saw—"

"Not right now!" Tom retorted. He hit the talk button on the radio once again. "Tank, bring the bus around for my guests, now!"

He stowed away the radio, sweat dripping from his brow, feeling even more harried. He walked to the end of the hallway and threw open another door and gestured for the group to move through the doorway. "Over here, folks. You're gonna love this."

The scowling businessman stepped forward and looked in the doorway. "This a toilet, Western-style."

Chapter 9

The crack of the bat against the ball pulled Tom out of his dark thoughts.

He was sitting in the stands at his son's early evening baseball game, hand on chin, totally absorbed in his own problems. Jimmy was about to bat, the helmet a little too big on his head, his arms holding the Louisville Slugger at an awkward sideways angle because he wasn't yet strong enough to hold it upward.

But he made contact. Tom felt another parent's hands seizing him by the arms, and he looked up just in time to see his son's home run arcing into the air and bouncing on the other side of the fence. He found himself shooting to his feet and applauding, then high-fiving everybody in sight as Jimmy came racing around third base, skipping, dancing, an ecstatic smile lighting up his face.

That was 'his' boy.

The game ended twenty minutes later with a narrow win for his son's team, and Jimmy leaped into his father's arms when it was finished.

"You did it!" said Tom. "Great hit!"

"Thanks, Daddy!"

He set his son down. "Now introduce me to the coach who taught you to swing like that."

His coach, standing nearby, overheard the conversation. "I didn't show him anything. It was that other guy—what did you say his name was?"

Jimmy shouted, "Tubby! Tubby showed me how to hit the ball!"

Tom winced. It should have been his job to teach Jimmy, but he was always so frustratingly busy . . .

They arrived home shortly before dark. Jimmy burst in the door before him, shouting to his mother about the home run that he had hit. Mary Anne was at the stove, stirring with a wooden spoon in the saucepot.

"Hi baby," he said, "I don't know what you're cooking, but it smells great."

"Hello," she replied.

He kissed her on the cheek. Something seemed a little bit off. He'd been married long enough to know his wife wasn't the type to hold onto her feelings for very long.

He took off his coat and sat down at the kitchen table. "What's up?"

"Pappy called again. He said he wants you to call him."

Tom felt panic sizzle through his stomach. "Why are you calling that man,

51

Pappy? I'm sure he had to be the same crank caller as before."

Mary Anne continued stirring the saucepot contents with the wooden spoon. She didn't say anything.

"He's not Pappy," he repeated. "Pappy has been dead for years."

"He seemed to know an awful lot about us. He knew about Ubercorn."

"Anybody can connect my name with Ubercorn," said Tom. He fought to control his voice a little. "I can't believe that imposter is still pretending to be Pappy."

"Pappy is really dead?"

"Deader than George Washington."

Mary Anne stirred the pot, then took it off the heat. "It's time to eat!" Mary Anne shouted to Jimmy. Tom noted a touch of anger lurking at the bottom of her voice.

Chapter 10

The phone call came from his business manager, John Gomez.

Tom had been in his office, kicked back, with his feet propped up on his desk, a toy model of Ubercorn's double-helix in his hands. A second later, he was leaning forward, feet on the floor, toy dropped to the floor. He switched the phone to the other ear.

"Tom," said Gomez's voice, "I don't know how to tell you this, but there's been a mutiny on the part of your investors. They're pulling out."

Suddenly, a huge booming sound echoed from the fields. Nearly jumping out of his pants, Tom peered out the window. That *boom* had been another massive strand of gray, dead corn falling over sideways.

"You're sure?" Tom said into the phone.

Gomez went on to say that not only had the Japanese investors been avoiding his phone calls, but so had the already-committed investors. "I got a certified letter from the lawyer representing all of them," he said, "and they're demanding their money back, voluntarily, or else they sue."

"On what grounds!" Tom shouted. "They invested in this idea, fair and square!"

"They'll find a loophole somewhere. The law firm they've got is one of the biggest sharks around. They'll find a piece of communication between our team and theirs, misinterpret it, and exploit it for all its worth. They received word that the corn was dying. They think there may have been a flaw in the hybridization or crossing and think it needs to be tested more and redeveloped successfully. Until then, they are out."

Tom squeezed his forehead with the fingers of his left hand. "We don't have the money to start over right now, and certainly not pay them back. It's all been sunk into this business."

"I'm really worried that you will lose everything, Tom."

"No!" Tom exclaimed, smashing his fist down onto the desk, then wincing. "It will not happen."

"I sincerely hope not, for your sake," said Gomez, "I sincerely do."

"So how long do we have?"

"As long as it takes to stave them off. Could be a month, could be a year. Get ready for some legal fees."

"I don't have that long." Tom buried his face between his knees. "Thanks,

Gomez."

"I'll send you an email later today with all the gory details."

Tom hung up the phone. He leaned backward in his seat and covered his eyes with his hands. He would not accept it was all hopeless.

"I have to do something," he said aloud, to nobody.

Tom stood up and went outside and down to the crop spray facility. An empty drum awaited filling. He began to unspool the hose from the rack to place in the drum. The hose caught tight on the rack. "Why is everything so difficult?" he muttered. He pulled with all his might to loosen it when he heard his son's voice.

"Daddy! Daddy! Mommy says to come quick!"

Surprised, he slung backward into the drum, and let go of the hose. It waved momentarily, slapping him in the legs, which were dangling just outside the drum. His arms and head rested on the other side, his body dropped inside the drum. He wiggled and scrambled to get out.

Jimmy ran in just in time to witness his struggles. He ran, laughing all the way, to help pull him out.

After finally being pulled from his unfortunate plight, Tom sprinted outside of the barn. His son was a few feet away, out of breath, having reverted to his panic state. He was pointing back to the house, where a pair of black SUVs had pulled up.

Standing in the middle of the commotion was the thin, precise figure of Mr. Withers. He stood peering around, as though he were afraid to move. Then he hesitantly took a couple of steps toward the porch. His assistant, Young Lin, bent down to wipe something off Withers's shoes. Mary Anne was standing on the porch with her hands on her hips, shouting something just out of Tom's recognizable hearing range.

Tom looked around. Four other men, all dressed in Mighty Bank of Elites polo shirts, emerged from the vehicles and fanned out across the property. They were photographing everything, the buildings, the crop duster, even the family dog.

"This is my property!" Tom shouted.

Tom ran across the dirt yard and up onto the porch. Withers looked at him the way you look at someone who hadn't bathed in a month, glancing up and down with disgust.

"Not for long," said Withers.

"I couldn't stop him," said Mary Anne. "They just drove up and got out."

"What are you hounds doing?" asked Tom.

Withers said, "Taking inventory. Now, Mr. Powers, this farm still belongs to the bank, at least until you can pay off the loan. After our little talk, I was less confident in it happening. Now, I've heard about the little insurrection on the part of your investors."

"How did you hear about that? I only just got the call."

The bank president held up his hand. "It's not called the Mighty Bank of Elites for nothing, Tom. We *talk to each other.*"

"So you've come to—"

"Assess the state of the property. It's preliminary. Nothing to be worried about." He nodded and gestured to his goons to go ahead and move. Tom spun around and caught sight of two of Withers's goons disappearing into the stalks of the Ubercorn.

"They can't go in there!" said Tom. "This is private property."

"Yes, and it's our private property," said Withers.

Mary Anne glared at him and quite sternly stated, "Not yet, it's not."

"Can we settle this some other way?" interjected Tom, to keep Mary contained. "Let's have dinner. Talk about this like grown men. Where would you like to go?"

"Mr. Withers doesn't usually dine with clients," interjected Young Lin.

An odd expression came across the bank president's face. "I admit that you can find me at the Salt Slab Steakhouse restaurant on most Friday nights. But those are meals reserved for my most important clients. Which you are definitely not."

"All right," Tom said. "That's it. It is still my property, Withers, so take your goons and vacate."

To make his point, Tom marched down the porch steps and thrust his face just inches from Withers's.

Withers blinked, stepped back, then said, "Fine, fine. We should be done anyway."

At that moment, the men came out of the field. They were carrying what looked to be cylindrical buckets. "Did you get the soil samples?" asked Withers.

"Yes sir," said one.

"All ready to go, sir."

"Very well," he replied.

"Wait! They can't do that," Tom exclaimed, then thought better of it. He needed this farm and had to convince Withers and the investors. His family depended on him.

Withers started to speak, but Tom stopped him.

"OK, I don't understand your methods, but I concede. We'll talk."

"I'm not sure it's possible," Withers replied turning away.

Jimmy, having frighteningly watched the encounter, spoke up. "Daddy, he's lying. I know it."

"Now son," Tom, looking back at his son, responded, "you need to stay out of this. I'll take care of it. If he's lying, it will come out sooner or later."

"But Daddy, I saw—"

"We'll talk later," Tom interrupted. "Right now, this man and his men need to leave."

Tom moved to stand with his family.

Withers turned to admire Tom, Mary Anne, and Jimmy, who stood tightly together with frowns on their faces. "Such an all-American tableaux." He clucked his tongue. "It will be a shame when you move into a rat-infested one-bedroom apartment in the big city. But that's what happens when you try something that is quite beyond your capabilities."

"Leave, now!" exclaimed Tom, keeping his anger in check.

Withers made a small wave with his hand, then turned. Young Lin made a perfunctory nod of the head, then ran around his boss and opened the door of the SUV.

Inside the SUV, Withers looked at the two goons with the buckets. "A brilliant plan, don't you think? They thought that you were collecting soil samples." He chortled briefly, shaking his head.

"Sir," said Young Lin, "may I ask what they were doing?"

"Spreading more worms," said Withers.

One of the goons opened his cylindrical bucket. It was empty. "They kill."

Withers tilted his head back and laughed. He knew he was just *this far* away from revenge on Pappy and his whole family. Finally, after all these years, he would get payback, with a few million in interest, alone.

Chapter 11

It was eight o'clock in the morning when Tom rolled up in his truck to the front of Pappy's mine. A sign read, Pappy's Chilly Mountain Salt Mine -- Outsiderz Keap Out! A hand-drawn skull underscored the intent.

He parked the vehicle and turned off the engine and stepped out. The entrance to the mine was a jumble of crude wooden beams with a rusted iron fence in front of it. An even cruder structure stood about a hundred yards away. It was made of scrap lumber and pieces of whatever else his father must have been able to scrounge up. This was apparently the office.

"It looks abandoned," he said to no one.

"Keep talkin' like that, you'ze gonna go 'bout hurtin' Pappy's feelin's," said a voice. The door banged open, and a tall man with dirty jeans and a slept-in camo shirt appeared in the doorway. His hair was a rat's nest, and his eyes squinted in the bright morning sunlight.

"Is Pappy here?" Tom asked.

"Depends who's askin'. Who 'er ya?"

"Pappy's son."

The man squinched his watery eyes again attempting to study Tom. He gazed up and down. It appeared as if the man was noting the similarities between Pappy and this man who claimed to be his son. Nodding approvingly, he stepped forward, tripped on the unseen threshold, and fell forward face-first in the dirt.

Tom moved to help the man when he heard Pappy's distant voice.

"Give 'im a minute."

Tom whirled, forgetting his task.

His father was moving toward him across the arid scrubland, walking stick in hand. "Dusty'll be fine. He's a little clumsy."

Sure enough, Dusty pulled himself to his feet, brushed himself off, and stumbled over to Tom. Pappy arrived at the same moment and clapped both men on the back. "Tommy, meet Dusty, my mine manager. Dusty, this's Tommy, my boy."

Tom hesitantly shook the manager's hand. It was slick with sweat, grease, and dirt. He discreetly wiped his hand on his jeans.

"My boy's here ta come see the mine," said Pappy. "Ya got my message the other day with no problem?"

"Pappy, please do not call me Tommy, and I really don't think you should call the house anymore."

Pappy looked sad. "But that woman who answered the phone has a mighty nice voice."

"That's my wife. I told her you were dead, but you keep calling. Now just stay dead."

Dusty laughed at that.

"All right, as ya wish," said Pappy. "Far be it from me ta interfere with your marriage. Now we're gonna head down just as soon as we get some paperwork completed."

"No, we're not," said Tom.

Pappy looked at him, crushed. "Why not? You've never seen it, not even one Mine Moppet—"

"Look, I just came over to tell you goodbye," said Tom.

Now his father seemed confused. "Are you leavin' ta go someplace? You cain't go on vacation, son. Runnin' a farm is a serious business, and ya don't get days off. It's like bein' a restaurant owner. Ya gotta be there, every day—"

Tom interrupted. "I'm not leaving the farm, Pappy. I'm just saying that we're not going to be seeing each other anymore. It's too much trouble. I'm already lying to my family about you. And I just frankly don't see the point."

"You was supposed ta help me," said his father. He gestured to the mine entrance. "We've got thousands a tons a rainbow salt in there that needs a buyer. I've got chili that sold a bunch, I mean, three thousand packs."

"Did it?" said Tom.

"It did! I just need a good, trustworthy team ta help me make more! And I've got a banker snappin' at my heels! And then, there's the Magical Mine Moppets."

"You really need to stop talking about them," said Tom. "People will know that you are crazy as a loon."

"Them'ze fer real, Tom!" shouted Dusty, holding a finger in the air as he stumbled back toward the office. "Believe it."

Tom ignored him. "Pappy, I tried to tell you otherwise, but you wouldn't listen. So let me be clear. This thing behind you, this dream of yours—it took you away from me. Forever. You understand?"

"Maybe."

"And it's just better if we weren't in each other's lives."

He looked into his father's eyes. They moved back and forth across Tom's face. "A'right then," Pappy finally said, "if that's what ya wish, then I cain't argue."

"I do wish. I wish that our relationship had been better so that it would be worth saving."

Tom turned and walked back toward his truck. He heard his father shout, "At least learn from this! Don't let it happen with your own son!"

Reaching his truck, Tom fumbled for his keys, thinking, *I'll never be like Pappy!*

Then he heard a sound at the entrance to the mine, then a weird laugh, a giggle really, seemed to come from inside the mine. Tom froze and stared back at the entrance, then he hopped into his truck. The laugh creeped him out, and he turned back for one more look at the mine.

Shaking it off, Tom started up the engine and drove away. It was just raccoon chattering, he told himself, funny little fellas that they are.

Chapter 12

In his penthouse office, Mr. Withers crouched in front of the dog cage. Inside was a tiny white Yorkshire terrier, wagging its tail fiercely, staring at the bank president as though he were about to toss a handful of beef jerky inside the cage. Withers had no such intention.

"Somebody brought this . . . animal into my building," he said with marked distaste.

The executive in the office shifted uncomfortably. "Yes, sir. The woman says that the dog is having health issues and that she needs to stay near him for the entire week."

"That is . . . pitiable," said Withers. He stuck a finger into the cage to lift up the dog's chin for a better look at him, but the animal snapped. He yanked his finger back.

He stood up suddenly. He had made a decision. "The employee keeps her job. She doesn't keep the animal. Young Lin!"

The closet door opened, and the assistant stepped out, his hair mussed up. "Yes, sir."

"Take this animal down to the shelter."

Young Lin looked at the animal. "Do you have that authority, sir?" He hemmed and hawed a bit more. "I mean, it's just that, well, it's not really your dog."

Withers wasn't in the mood for an argument. "Get that dog out of this building."

He obediently picked up the cage and carried it out of the room.

Withers looked at the executive and shrugged. "Tell her that she deserves a healthy animal. Nature takes care of the sick in its own unique way."

The executive nodded and left the room. Withers sat in his swivel seat behind his desk, finger on his chin, thinking. Then, making sure that nobody was looking, he reached into a hidden drawer in his desk and removed a framed photo. It was aging and faded, and the black-and-white photo featured himself as a young man with his arm around a young woman. He felt his lip tremble as he studied the photo.

Then a spasm of rage coursed through him. He threw the photo into the drawer and slammed it shut. Just more bad memories, and just more motivation to pay back Pappy. He picked up his phone and hit the intercom to his secretaries. "All of you, get my bodyguards in here. And get Young Lin. I want him here, too."

Young Lin reappeared in the office with the dog cage in hand. The four goons followed and stood around Withers's desk. The bank president took in the cage and pointed to the exterior. "Keep that thing out there. We are trying to start a meeting."

Young Lin put the dog down outside the office and went back inside. He produced his notebook and with more than a hint of weariness in his voice said, "Yes sir."

"We," began Withers, "by which, of course, I mean I, have decided the time has come for payback. Pappy must pay."

"For what, sir?" said one of the goons.

With a blank stare at the green lampshade on his desk, Withers entered a deep sub-conscious state. A vivid picture appeared as he remembered a time some many years before . . .

Young Withers kept a tight grip on the rolled-up, rubber-banded newspapers. He couldn't believe that his dad still made him deliver papers at sixteen years old.

His dad sat next to him behind the wheel. "Some of those other papers look kind of sloppy like you didn't take the time to roll them up real tight."

"They're tight enough," Withers said.

"Are you back talking me?"

Withers looked away, out the window at the corn fields they were whizzing by and rolled his eyes. "No, sir."

"Better not be! Your backside should still be sore from last night's lickin', but I won't hesitate to whack ya a good one again."

"Yessir." He saw ahead the farm where his classmate lived. "We're coming up on Pappy's farm, Dad."

"Man, what kind of name is that for a kid? Pappy?"

"His mother loved the name Pepé, but he hates it. Everybody called him Pepé Le Pew."

"Well," his dad mumbled. "I could see why he wouldn't like to be named after a cartoon skunk."

"Yessir, there he is, ahead, behind the plow."

"Danged sodbuster!" Withers's dad exclaimed, laughing. "Hey, I got a buck that says you can't bean that farm boy with that paper!"

"A buck?"

"Yep!"

"It's in the bank!" Withers leaned way out of the window, keeping a bead on Pappy.

"Let 'er rip, boy!"

Withers flung the paper hard, but it landed some thirty feet away from Pappy, who heard the thump of the newspaper hitting the dirt, and turned for a look at them.

"Hah! You always did throw like a little girl," Withers's dad said. "Pay up, loser!"

Withers sagged. He hated that he couldn't throw well, or do anything athletic for that matter, despite his dad's wishes that he become a pro ballplayer. He reached into his pants and extracted a damp dollar bill and placed it into his dad's outstretched palm.

"Ha! A buck earned is a buck saved," his dad said. "Shoot, though. I sure would've liked to see you bean that sodbuster right on the melon!"

"Yessir," he replied, wanting to please his dad. Although his aim fell a little short because unbeknownst to his dad, Pappy was his best friend.

"Say, hey! You are the one taking that pretty little Iris girl to the dance, right?"

Withers perked up. His dad didn't try to be nice and cheer him up very often. "Yessir! No way she'd be going with that sodbuster cartoon skunk!"

He and his dad shared a rare laugh together.

Withers hadn't told his dad the truth. That pretty little Iris girl was the daughter of the mayor of Borough Falls. Withers had moved to town in the sixth grade and from the moment he'd seen her sashay through the door of their geography classroom, he had known one thing, for certain.

Iris would be his.

Someday.

Withers told his best friend, over and over again, about his plans for Iris. Pappy usually just nodded or offered a word about how pretty and how nice Iris was, but not much more.

One year after her father had taken office, Iris's mother died. Withers went to the funeral with all the other classmates. Then he went to the reception in the family home, a towering mansion on the hill. He stayed around after the reception, trying to offer his support. She didn't tell him to leave.

Soon he became a frequent guest in the mayor's house, visiting Iris. He didn't mind the thirty-minute walk to see his princess on the highest hill overlooking Borough Falls. He trudged up the wide steps to their grand porch, dropping his head. Just think, Walter Withers, a mere peasant, visiting the girl of his dreams. It didn't matter that he had to sit on the sofa with his hands crossed and listen to her talk about nothing for hours.

He was in love.

Iris seemed to love him too. She had told Withers she loved him being there. It was because of who he was, not because of how much money his family did or didn't have. She talked of future marriage, and Iris's maids scampered about whenever he entered the house. One hag, the head of the maid staff, was skeptical, giving him the old stink eye whenever he entered. Still, she was no real obstacle, and Withers went to bed every night, dreaming of a future he'd never thought was possible before.

Then Withers decided to make it official.

He came to see his princess in her house overlooking Borough Falls and asked her to marry him. Iris seemed pleased, but she asked for a ring. Withers told her that he didn't have a ring, that he couldn't provide her with the lifestyle.

That night he attempted to steal a ring. Withers had seen it, a fancy vivid blue diamond almost fifteen carats, in a shop downtown. His greed overtook his reason as he smashed the case, took the ring, and fled. It was a childish gesture, an amateur job, and they caught him a few hours later. Withers came clean immediately. The mayor talked with his parents, who lowered their heads in shame at the news. He had become a thief. Nobody cared that he was young and in love. He had only stolen because his heart was stolen. He wanted to win Iris's heart and make her see how much he truly loved her. Her father was not forgiving. Withers was ejected from paradise.

That night his dad drove him away, to a different town, a different school, where he would finish his high school education. He vowed to return to Borough Falls someday with a real ring, paid for, beg forgiveness of Iris and her family, and gain their trust. Withers felt his princess would forgive him, with time. They would not keep him away forever.

Withers asked Pappy to befriend Iris, to make sure she was all right, until his return. He hadn't counted for her to fall in love with Pappy!

His best friend had charmed Iris with his tall tales and his crazy plans. Two years later, he'd asked for her hand in marriage. Iris said yes.

Withers raged, cried out, and cursed Pappy. The day of their wedding, he made plans to return to Borough Falls, to seek revenge upon the town that had wronged him and had destroyed his dreams. In the years that followed, he worked hard, gained prestige, power, and wealth. He returned and founded the Mighty Bank of Elites, and constructed it with the same flight of steps that he remembered climbing up to Iris's mansion, except this time much longer. There was no way the low scum in society could ever enter those grand halls.

All for the love of a girl. And all to get back at that skunk, Pappy and all those men who denied him access to the girl who stole his heart.

Withers suddenly realized that he was still staring at the green lampshade on his desk, his men waiting uncomfortably for his next utterance.

"He stole my girl!"

"He what, sir?"

Withers leaped to his feet. "He stole my girl! Married her!"

"There's a lot of other girls, Mr. Withers."

"At least a thousand," added another goon.

"No, there aren't any other women!" Withers spat. "I wanted that one. She was mine. And that lunatic came along—and he just, just, just charmed her right away from me. And then he married her!"

Withers's hand clenched into a fist. He wanted to whack that Pappy with it. "There is a clause in Pappy's mortgage that allows the bank to foreclose in the event of something called *mental incompetency on the part of the operator*. And this old fool and his imaginary 'Magical Mine Moppets' are just the ticket for us. Questions?"

The goons shook their heads. He stared at the four men. Man, they were dullards.

"You are all dismissed."

Chapter 13

Back at the Powers farm, Mary Anne sat in the family study, looking over the books. The tip of her pencil skirted the edge of a long list of numbers in the ledger. Her fingertips danced over a calculator. The final number came up.

She sat back and sighed. "I don't know how we're going to do this."

She rose and decided to take a trip over to speak with Tom at his office. She grabbed the leash and called Bojangles, the dog. There was no noise. "He must be exploring somewhere. I'll have to remember to look later," she thought. She opened the back door and headed for the office.

Tom was at his desk when Mary Anne walked in.

"Come on, why don't you close up for the night. Let's take a walk," she said. "We have to talk about the payment."

"Don't remind me."

A few minutes later, Tom and Mary Anne walked back toward the house. "Tom, we can't make the payment."

"I know," he said.

"Is there any way you can persuade Withers to give us just one more month?"

He thought about it. "What day is tomorrow?"

"Friday."

He thought about it. "I can try a different way of approaching him, but I don't know if it'll work."

Chapter 14

Tom pulled into the parking lot of the cavernous restaurant, above it, a neon sign with a kitschy cow stretched out seductively on an oversized table with the words *Salt Slab* Steakhouse above it. The valet guys ran back and forth as people poured in and out, dressed to the nines. Tom decided to park his own car way in the back where there were plenty of spots.

Tom could smell the crisp linens and breadsticks on the tables before entering the front door. Crystal wine glasses clanked and servers cruised between tables. Tom straightened up and adjusted his tie.

"Reservation for Tom Powers," he lied to the teenaged hostess.

She shuffled through some papers and then looked up with confident brown eyes. "I don't see that name on my list, sir."

Tom leaned over her podium and casually dropped a one hundred dollar bill in front of her. "Would you mind looking one more time?"

Her mouth dropped open. She looked left, then right, then stuffed the bill in her pocket. "Right this way," she said, grabbing a menu.

He scoured the dining room. He recognized Withers. "Excuse me, is that Withers over there?" he asked the hostess.

"Yes!" she said, a little too excited. "Do you know Mr. Withers?"

"Sort of. I see an empty table for two in that corner near Withers's table. May I be seated there?"

"Most certainly," she responded.

After being seated and given a menu, he began contemplating his strategy. He quickly realized he was close enough to their table to hear what Withers and his date were discussing. He put his menu up and leaned in.

He could see the earnest expression on Withers's face as he attempted to charm her.

"I must say, Marcia, no woman can compare to your rare beauty. Your name, your eyes, your very essence, is intoxicating. It's an honor to be sitting here with you."

"My name's Kendra," his date said, not looking up from her nails. *Wow*, Tom thought, *he's trying way too hard*. He almost couldn't wait for more of this train wreck to unfold.

"That's a beautiful name, Kendra," Withers went on. "I would love to buy you dessert. Anything on the menu for someone as special as you."

Withers hadn't a clue, and his date seemed bored in his presence. The awkwardness gave Tom a deep sense of satisfaction. Withers might win in the game with Pappy, but he was certainly losing when it came to women.

Kendra picked up the menu, looked at it for three seconds and dropped it down to her lap. "Flan," she said.

"What a coincidence; that's what I want, too. If you see the waiter, please let him know. I'm headed to the men's room. Back in two shakes of a lamb's tail." Withers got up and headed toward the bathroom.

Kendra let out a sigh of relief and took her phone from her purse. This was it, Tom realized.

Just as he was about to rise, the server approached Tom's table. "Good evening, sir, and welcome to Salt Slab Steakhouse. Have you dined with us before?"

"Yeah," Tom said, getting up. "Gimme a bloody ribeye." He headed to the men's room and walked in with his new plan in the works to find Withers exiting a stall and heading to the sink. Tom casually sidled up to the sink next to him and began washing his hands.

Withers stretched out his hands toward the attendant, then cleared his throat. The man jumped to his feet and squirted hand soap into the banker's soft hands.

Tom turned to look at him. "Why, it's Mr. Withers. What are you doing here?"

"Having dinner with somebody."

"It's Tom Powers. Remember me?"

The bank president wore a sour look on his face. "Of course."

"Hey, as long as we're here," said Tom, "is there any way to get just one more month extension on my payment?"

Withers snarled. "You have had many extensions, Mr. Powers. There will be no more."

Tom fought the urge to comment on this and decided to stick with the plan he'd created a few minutes earlier. "I couldn't help noticing you were having a bit of trouble with your lady friend."

"Trouble?" Withers asked, checking out his teeth in the mirror. "I think she's quite attracted to me."

"No offense, but she can't wait to get away from you. Let me make you an offer—if I show you how to talk to her, and if it works, you'll give me that extension." He leaned forward. "You could've used my help when my father stole my mother away from you."

Tom hit a nerve. Withers barely contained his anger, then seemed to will himself to calm down. He turned away from the sink and accepted a towel from the attendant.

"Fine," he said.

"First, you're too complimentary. Women like her don't care."

"What should I be?"

Tom began to give him a spiel on being charming to women, how not to sound desperate and cloying. "Well, first off, you find yourself a nice girl, not a cold-hearted gold digger like that. But since you wish to be with somebody like her, be sure to know her name. Find out what she's interested in. Get her to talk. Act interested in her. Forget the vain compliments. She already thinks she's all that. It means nothing to her. Boring. Tell her about you. Play off of her interests. Don't talk about other women. Reach out and touch her hand, gently."

"I'll think about it," Withers replied.

"I can help you. I'll even prompt you."

"All right, but you had better be right."

"I will. Just follow my lead."

They developed a plan and returned to their respective tables, where Tom's bloody steak awaited and two flans sat on Withers's table.

He looked over at Withers motioning for him to start. He listened as well as he could over the noise of the increasingly crowded restaurant as Withers began following his men's room instructions. At each part, when Withers cued him, he played charades to lead the conversation.

Withers had just reached out his hand and touched Kendra's when she looked at him, shocked, and pulled away. She suddenly yelled, "I know what you want! I don't even know what came over me to date an old man. You can't even have a meaningful conversation without help. You are hopeless! You think it's that easy to get a girl to like you just because of your money. I would never marry a man like you if he were the richest man alive!" She glanced in Tom's direction, collected her purse and coat and left.

After she had gone, Withers wiped the dessert off his suit. Then he came and stood over Tom, glowering with anger.

"You must have done it wrong," said Tom.

Withers looked at him mercilessly, without explaining himself. "Your payment is due in two weeks."

"But I can't come up with the money by then."

"Tough. You and that Pappy of yours are through, bucko. Through! That skunk you call a father cost me everything once. But I intend to get it all back and then some!"

Withers pivoted on his heel and was gone.

"This guy is out to ruin both of us!" Tom exclaimed.

Chapter 15

A few minutes after dawn, Tom rolled up to Pappy's Chilly Mountain Salt Mine and parked in front of the ramshackle office.

Before exiting his truck, he sat thinking about the trip to Slab's and his disastrous encounter with Withers. He couldn't fathom why Withers would want to destroy both father and son. "I don't even want to be associated with Pappy," he thought. He had entered into a loan agreement with Withers in spite of his father, but he now wished he had not done so. He remembered the words of his mother as she told him about Withers and why he should not receive a loan from the Mighty Bank of Elites.

"Now Tommy," she said, "Withers can help you, that is certain, but you understand he is ruthless. He was removed from this town when he made some poor choices. My father did not want a scandal. He was the mayor after all. It was better that he just left. Then your dad helped me get through this most difficult time. He was so kind, affectionate, and mostly just witty and whimsical. I just fell in love with him. Withers found out your dad married me. He still never showed up since he was banned, but after my father and all the men involved in his departure were gone, he returned. He opened the bank of Elites, for only the richest men around these parts and beyond. Your dad had been trying to get the local bank to give him a loan on the mine. Withers heard about it, and he went to your dad. He pretended that he was sorry and was highly interested in your dad's endeavors. I think he was trying to see how he could ruin your dad. I think he saw an ambitious man who would fail at gaining anything from an old mine and he could hang him and prove to me that he was the better man. I truly love Pappy and would never give Withers the satisfaction of destroying his life and our family. No matter what, Pappy will always be a better man than Withers. In any case, Withers gave him the loan. Then your dad began to spend hours, then days, and weeks at the mine. Soon Withers found out he was often gone. He began to show up at places around town wherever I was. He tried luring me away from Pappy. I never gave in, and he started to change drastically. He began to be ruthless, in words and actions. Not only me, but the entire town, began to suffer from his revenge."

It was his undoing. He should have believed his mother when she had warned him about Withers. Now he was put in a position to find out Withers's reasoning behind him wanting to destroy his livelihood. Understandably, he was his father's son, but as his father had been out of the picture for a very long time, it seemed Withers would have been over the whole ordeal.

Maybe he could somehow work with Pappy to uncover Withers's malicious intent to destroy him and ultimately save the farm, even if this meant agreeing to help Pappy save his mine to get his cooperation.

He exited the truck and walked to the mine office door.

He knocked on the door and waited. Eventually, it swung open. Dusty stood there, resplendent in a ripped white t-shirt with oil stains on the belly. A filthy mining suit was unrolled to his waist, and Wellingtons were parked on his feet.

"Dusty, good morning. I need to see Pappy."

He pointed to his left eye. "So does I, but this un's still a bit blurry-eyed. In fact, you'ze a big ol' piece uh fuzz right 'bout now. Who're youz?"

"It's Tom. Where is my father?"

"He done spent the whole night in that thar mine. Them Mine Moppets was havin' some kind a family gatherin'. Racket kept me up fer tha longest dog-gone time."

Tom heard the gate to the mine squeak open. He glanced over and saw Pappy emerge from the mine. He looked energized, and his eyes were filled with some kind of wildfire.

Tom left the small ramshackle office and approached his father.

"Proof that I have a magnetic personality," his father said, "'cause here ya are, drawn ta me once again."

"Pappy—"

"Why'd ya come back? Ya aren't supposed ta even know me."

Tom sighed, exasperated with life. "Because I think we're in the same situation."

"How's that?"

"The bank is trying to repossess the things that mean the most to us. Your mine, my farm."

Pappy's nose twitched while he thought about that. "Ya already met Withers?"

"Several times. He hates me."

"That's 'cause I stole your mother away from 'im, or so he says. She was plenty done with Withers, that's fer certain as a baby monkey knows his own mama. He could never let it go, always complainin'. I hope he learned how ta talk ta women."

"He didn't," said Tom, "trust me. So let me tell you about what's going on."

They walked together across the scrubland, and Tom related everything—

falling behind on payments, talking to Withers in his office, Withers's visit to the farm, and finally his encounter in the steakhouse.

When Tom finished, Pappy chewed on his lower lip. "We really are in the same boat, and we're sinkin.'"

"Yeah," Tom said. Tom hoped he had not made a mistake, but he knew if he did not raise Pappy from the dead, somehow his family would find out his secret and it could destroy everything he had ever worked or lived for. He knew it was time, "You better come meet everybody."

Pappy turned to him, beaming. "So that means we can finally meet! That'll be wonderful. We'll be a happy family!"

Tom held up a warning hand. "There are conditions on our relationship. One, we are only going to help each other save ourselves from Withers. No promises beyond that. And two, no talk about Magical Mine Moppets!"

His father looked at him. "Ya still don't believe in 'em?"

"I don't have to not believe in them. They don't exist."

Pappy thought about it, then shrugged. "It's hard ta believe the existence of anythin' we've never seen. Right now, we gotta get saved."

Chapter 16

Tom pulled up in his driveway dreading the encounter with Mary Anne and Jimmy.

He knew he should just come clean about Pappy. But every way he had thought about telling Mary Anne just confused him more. So he had just doubled down on his lie, as much as it troubled him to do so. Now he had to tell her about him. She just didn't need to know everything.

He saw her in the side garden. He stepped out of his truck and called out. "I've got big news!"

She was peering at her violets, inspecting them. "Really?"

Often, when Tom had "big news" it turned out to be just another harebrained scheme of his, and he realized that Mary Anne had become pretty blasé about his breathless announcements.

"It's Pappy. My father's alive, and he's coming to visit!"

"What? But you told he was dead trying to rescue—""—a squirrel from a threshing machine."

"So he wasn't killed?"

"I never saw the body!"

"So they lied to you?"

"Yes! Can you believe it? Those crumbs I once called my family lied to me!"

"No wonder you don't speak to them."

"That's all behind me now. My father is alive and coming to visit!"

Turning to him, she smiled, something he was glad to see. "Well, that's the way it should be Tom."

As usual, she was right. "Yes," he said, "it should."

Jimmy ran out of the house. His hair wasn't combed, and the sun was burning the sleep from his eyes. "Mommy, Daddy, what's happening?"

"Son," said Tom. He wondered how to tell the boy the truth. Then he just said it. "You won't believe this, but your grandfather is alive."

"Pappy? He's alive?"

Tom nodded. "He's been alive all this time. He had no mercy on squirrels. And that's what kept him alive! It was all a lie. Don't you understand?"

"No."

"Of course you don't! The important thing is, he wants to meet you." He accentuated the pronoun with a friendly poke to the boy's chest.

"But you said he was dead!"

"Yeah, about that . . . I know I did. And I will explain everything to you, OK? But right now we have to get ready for Pappy to visit!"

"Can we get a cake to celebrate?" Jimmy's eyes glistened with hope.

"I don't see why not," said Tom, and Jimmy grinned and ran off.

Tom cast a sideways glance at Mary Anne, and she didn't look happy.

"I'm going to tell him everything! Soon."

Mary Anne caught Tom's eye, and she was very stern-looking, like, *You better tell him the truth.*

Three hours later, Mary Anne and Jimmy walked through the front door with a large sheet cake from the local grocery store. The plastic top displayed an intricately decorated picture of a squirrel with the words *Welcome Home Pappy!* circling it.

Everyone looked their best. Jimmy's hair was parted and slicked down, Mary Anne wore her best flowered dress, and Tom kept a sport coat on despite the heat. The three of them stood, silently, and peered down the long driveway, dead cornstalks dancing across it with every gust of wind.

A large cloud of dust formed around the gate and moments later, a figure emerged from it. He walked toward the farm. Really slowly.

As he approached, Tom stepped off the porch and walked down the drive to meet him. His lips held tight with emotion, he leaned forward and hugged his father, haltingly. Then he pulled back quickly. Pappy's eyes were moist.

"First hug in twenty years," he said.

"I know," said Tom. He looked down at his father's shoes and pants, which were covered in dust. "Did you walk here?"

"Of course. Gotta stay young."

Pappy hummed to himself, skipped, and danced as he moved down the tall walls of dead corn. He approached the Powers farmhouse.

On the porch, Jimmy was rapt. "Is that him, Mommy?"

"Your guess is as good as mine. Pappy?"

Pappy raised a hand. He spun around 360 degrees, as though in a pirouette, faced them, then bowed deeply.

Jimmy's eyes lit up. "Pappy!" He ran forward, off the porch and hugged the old man.

Mary Anne wasn't far behind. She embraced Pappy warmly. "Pappy, Tom has told me so much about you—"

"And I've heard absolutely nothin' 'bout you."

"Tell me what happened with the squirrel, Pappy!" Jimmy excitedly exclaimed.

"Squirrel?"

"Forget the squirrel. Pappy, this is my wife, Mary Anne, and my son, Jimmy," announced Tom.

"It's a pleasure to finally meet you," responded Mary Anne, politely.

"And a pleasure ta be back from the grave," he joked.

"Let me show you around before we have some lunch," said Tom.

The Powers' home was a one-hundred-year-old farmhouse with creaks, cracks, and scuffed-up wooden furniture. Mary Anne and Tom had worked hard to make the place look cozy and welcoming with colorful rugs and simple window treatments, but they couldn't mask that underlying shabby look.

Pappy strolled through the house like it was an art gallery, marveling at every room. He stopped at a blank wall. "Oh, that's nice. That's a good un," he said as if he had just noticed a really nice work of art.

"Pappy, that's a blank wall," Tom replied.

"I like the contourin'."

Tom shook his head. He instructed everyone to find their way to the kitchen table for lunch. The four of them took their seats—Jimmy and Mary Anne with big smiles on their faces, while Tom looked as though he'd just completed a marathon. Mary Anne had prepared cornbread, corn chowder, creamed corn, and of course, corn on the cob, all of which looked delicious despite the withering stalks outside.

Pappy dove in and methodically sprinkled salt over Jimmy's meal. He turned to Jimmy. "Now you do the same for me, son."

Jimmy was careful to apply just the right amount, clearly desiring Pappy's approval. Tom worried even more with this.

Pappy beamed at the boy. "You're quite adept with that shaker," he said.

"He loves salt," Mary Anne said.

Tom couldn't help himself. "He must get it from Pappy there," he said, a little too loudly. "Salt is the most important thing in the world to him." Tom couldn't hide the anger in his voice.

Either Pappy didn't have a combative bone in his body, or he was as clueless as ever. He nodded and agreed, "Salt *is* important."

Tom stood up, "Yeah, *to you*! More important than family or me or anyone, huh?"

The table fell silent.

"Pappy, I tuck my son into bed every night. I read to him. I ask him how his day was. I play baseball with him. We have a relationship."

But when he looked at his wife and son, they just stared back at him. He was confused—why didn't they back him up on this?

Pappy looked at Mary Anne and Jimmy. "What do they know about my life?" he asked Tom.

"Nothing."

Pappy, still seemingly unfazed by Tom's attack, picked up the salt shaker once again and sprinkled a pinch of salt into his fingers. He held it out to Jimmy, who voluntarily cupped his hands to catch it before hitting the table. "I mine this. Salt. I have a salt mine. And the sad truth is I sorta ignored your daddy ta pursue that dream when he was just a child. He didn't do anythang wrong. I had a dream, and I followed it. Even though it meant leavin' others behind most a the time."

Tom couldn't decide if this was an apology or simply a narration. "Tell them the rest, Pappy," he pushed.

Pappy folded his hands atop the table and said, "It's a special salt. Rare salt." And then he had a gleam in his eye. "Magic salt."

Jimmy perked up. "Magic salt?"

"I use it in my product, Pappy's Chilly Mountain Chili Mix. Three thousand units sold."

Tom asked, "Yeah? Who're your customers?"

"That I cain't tell ya. The store just tells me they done sold out. I think it could become enormous. Have a look." He reached behind him to produce a small package that looked like the kind Mary Anne used to season the meat on taco night, but this one was bright green and displayed a giant version of Pappy's weathered face with that oblivious grin. "Voila!" he handed the package to Jimmy. "Now, ya take good care a this. It's very valuable."

Jimmy accepted the gift and inspected the front and back. "Mommy, can we try it?"

Mary Anne nodded.

"Right now?" Jimmy coaxed.

"Tomorrow," she replied.

Jimmy had stars in his eyes and suddenly wanted to know every detail. "Do you work in the salt mine by yourself?"

Tom knew this was coming. His entire body tensed with anticipation of Pappy's answer. How could he stop him without creating a scene?

"I have help from some friends who live down in the mine."

"That's enough, Pap—." Tom couldn't stop him.

"The Magical Mine Moppets," Pappy said.

Inside Tom's brain was a sound like pots and pans falling down the stairs.

"The what?" Jimmy asked.

"The Magical Mine Moppets," Pappy said.

"Oh, I think I know one," said Jimmy.

"What makes ya say that? Ya ever been ta the mine? I didn't know I'd had company and not known it."

"No, it's just I have this friend, she's a bug. Her name is Lacey. She told me so. Well, not in words, just in writing. She talks with her feet."

"Well, I'm not sure 'bout that. Never met a 'Lacey' downside. The Mine Moppets don't leave. The king won't let 'em. It's dangerous, ya know."

"OK. But I really think she is sure special."

"I'm sure she is. Mine Moppets are all shapes and sizes. Next time I go downside I sure will ask. It'd be a pleasant surprise to know one of themz been upside."

Finally having had enough of this imaginary talk of Mine Moppets and talking creatures, Tom picked up the half-eaten ear of corn from his plate and then threw it down again. Then he snatched the package of chili mix from Jimmy's hands and shoved it into his own pocket. "Lunch is over. Time for your nap!"

"Daddy, I'm nine! I don't take naps."

"Then go do your homework." Tom pointed toward the hallway, and Mary Anne took Jimmy to his room.

Tom sunk down at the now empty table. "The Magical Mine Moppets? Really?"

"They're still real." Pappy folded his arms.

He'd been spinning this yarn as long as Tom could remember and it was time to let it go. "We had an agreement," said Tom.

"I'm sorry, I forgot."

"You were talking about them when I was six years old. I thought I could believe you, then I learned I couldn't, and I don't believe you now. Why do you keep lying about these things?"

"I wasn't lyin' then, and I'm not lyin' now. Maybe you think your son is lyin' too?"

"My son is not lying. He just has a vivid imagination. He loves to explore, just like any kid does."

"Well I tell ya, I don't just see things. They exist. Maybe ya should find out for yaself. I always wanted ya to."

"That's enough! You and your delusions!"

Tom needed some air. He turned and headed out the front door and stood on the porch and stared at his dying corn. Talking to his father was like talking to a wall. Maybe it had been better to keep Pappy "dead." It was a horrible thought, but Tom wasn't sure about anything anymore. Tom put his hand in his pocket, felt the package he took from Jimmy and walked down the steps toward the granary. He reached the door and looked around. Seeing no one, he entered and again looked around inside. Finding it empty, he headed to the far back corner. A small pile of corn had been pushed against the wall, and he began to push away the kernels. Soon, he revealed a small hidden door, with no handle, in the wall. He opened it, and the aroma from inside began to permeate outside the small room that was disclosed. He bent down and crawled through the door into a small room just large enough to kneel inside. He turned on the light from his cell phone. He pulled out the package in his pocket, just about to lay it with the others when the room suddenly filled with Pappy's face and a strong sense of his presence. His eyes unexpectedly filled with tears. Unsure of exactly what feelings he was experiencing, he knew one thing, he could not bring himself to place this new package into the chili tomb. Stuffing the package back in his pocket, he crawled out and shut the door. He quickly covered the area with the removed corn kernels and proceeded to leave the granary.

Suddenly, out of the corner of his eye, he saw a small shadowy figure in a corner near the front. He cautiously moved toward it. As he neared, the little shadow jumped up into the light, making him jump back in surprise. It was just the family dog shaking his body and wagging his tail.

"What are you doing in here, Bojangles? You know Mary Anne will be upset to find you in here. Come on, let's get out of here before she finds us."

Tom, with Bojangles on his heels, left the granary and headed back to the house.

Chapter 17

Late that evening, after the drama settled and Pappy had gone home, Tom went off to his office at the administration building.

Mary Anne was busy cleaning up. There was nobody in the house except, Bojangles. She looked down at the animal. He looked back at Mary Anne expectantly, tail wagging. With everything that had been going on around the farm, his walks had been neglected, along with his belly rubs.

"I'll take you out in a minute," she said, then finished setting the table for the next meal.

She turned back to the butler's pantry to remove plates when she heard footsteps on the porch. The door opened, and Jimmy entered the house. She could hear him standing in the doorway, taking off his shoes.

"Hi Mommy!" he said.

"Hey, baby. Bojangles is a little frisky, sweetie, be sure to close the door."

The dog went sprinting over to the door. She heard Jimmy giggle as the dog reached him. Then she heard Jimmy shout, "No!"

Mary Anne shot out of the dining room. She could see Jimmy still holding the door open, one shoe on his foot and the other shoe in his hand, looking out into the dark fields.

"I couldn't stop him!" the boy said. "He just ran past me!"

"Oh no," she said. Bojangles was a good dog, but Mary Anne knew from prior experience that corralling him was next to impossible, and he could get himself into mischief. She threw on her shoes, grabbed her jacket and the leash, and ran out the door, calling back to Jimmy, "Stay here just in case Bojangles comes back!"

The dark night air was cool on her skin. "Bojangles! Come back here!"

A distant woof reached her ear, followed by another. She followed the sonar. It appeared that the dog was hightailing it for the granary.

"I can help!" Jimmy called from inside.

"No! Do your homework!" Mary Anne yelled, already running. To the dog: "Bojangles! Come back here!"

At the granary, an Ubercorn worker stepped out of the door . . . and the dog slipped past him and dashed inside.

"For Pete's sake!" Mary Anne sighed. "Hold the door!"

She ran into the granary, where there were towering piles of corn everywhere. The thick, suffocating smell enveloped her head. She hit the light switch and moved down the central aisle as the florescent overhead lights lit up the spacious room.

"Bojangles!" she shouted. "Where are you? Come here!"

Another bark. There: she spotted him. Near the far wall, happy as a pig in slop, the family dog was digging furiously into a pile of corn, tail wagging away.

"Bojangles! Get out of there!" Mary Anne shouted. She approached him from behind, grabbed his collar and pulled him back, but the dog lunged forward again. "What are you looking for?"

Suddenly he stopped digging and started sniffing. Mary Anne spotted a wooden door peeking out from behind the mound of corn. "What in the world are you doing?"

Bojangles stood next to her, proud of his discovery. She slowly popped open the door and peeked inside. It was dark. She went back to the front of the granary and grabbed the emergency flashlight. She returned and entered the small room. It was a chamber full of packages, thousands of them. She picked one up and looked at it. The label read *Pappy's Chilly Mountain Chili Mix*.

"Oh, my!" she exclaimed.

Mary Anne marched into Tom's office and hurled a handful of chili packets on his desk. "Three thousand packs of chili mix?" She was out of breath, and her hair looked like she'd spent an hour riding in a convertible. Tom was caught off guard, but he knew he had better speak up sooner rather than later.

"Three thousand and one," he mumbled. "That would be including the one Pappy gave us."

"Why didn't you tell me about this?" "Because you thought he was dead." Tom felt like a child having been caught stealing candy.

"But you knew, *the entire time*, he was alive?"

He wanted to disappear into the floor. "Yes, as far as I knew."

"Which means you lied to me." Mary Anne sat down and folded her arms tightly.

"Honey, my father is an embarrassment. It was easier to pretend that he was dead. I didn't want you to know he abandoned me for a mine filled with imaginary magical creatures."

She raised her voice. "*You lied to me*! Over and over and over again!"

"Mary Anne, I am so sorry. I was embarrassed by Pappy. And once I got that lie started, I didn't know how to stop it. I just keep adding lies on top of it.

I'm so sorry."

Tom knew it wasn't enough. A marriage was supposed to be built on love and trust, but his lie had continued for several years. What sort of example was this to their son? How could he get Mary Anne to understand that once the lie started, it was practically impossible to stop?

"But for years, I wasn't sure if he was alive or not so I just made him die. I fabricated the squirrel story. No one was the wiser. Then I heard about him a few years ago, when he started trying to sell his chili mix."

"Why did you buy all that stuff?" she asked.

Tom sighed, "I guess I thought if I helped my father somehow, that maybe someday he'd appear, maybe happy that he had finally made his fortune, and wanted to tell someone, namely me. I just wanted a dad, not some man who appeared a few times here and there, then disappeared again. The last time, forever. I just wanted him to love me again."

He meant that, and Mary Anne must have known it—and it clearly touched her. She softened. "You don't think he loves you?"

"I don't know."

"I think he does, in his own weird way. I saw that today. When was the last time you saw him?"

"Twenty years ago and then right after his first phone call to the house."

She regarded her husband, and Tom could sense her internal war between anger and sympathy. Now she knew, and though she was still mad, it was a mighty weight off Tom's shoulders. He realized that, when it came to telling the truth, it was always best to do so right away, but if you don't for some reason, well, come clean as soon as possible.

Finally, she walked over and hugged him. "I'm still not sure if I should forgive you."

He looked up at her. "I wouldn't forgive me."

"Even if you don't deserve forgiveness, we have to fix this. We have to work together. I love you and will stand by you all the way. Family is important."

Tom looked at Mary Ann. He vowed to fix this. She was right. Family was important. He just didn't realize it until now. He was in a mess.

Chapter 18

Tom moved the glasses of ice water aside and spread out the paperwork on the table at the diner. He had met Pappy inside Madge's Diner, and he was showing Pappy his loan agreement from the Mighty Bank of Elites. Tom believed that if they compared agreements, they might be able to find some inconsistencies that would help make their case stronger. If that didn't work, if it yielded no insights as to how to save their properties, then he figured that they would have to hire a lawyer.

"See here," he said, the tip of his pencil touching a paragraph on the fourth page, "it says here that pursuant to the collateral there's a grace period of sixty days before anything is reported to credit bureaus. Pursuant to the collateral."

Pappy looked lost. "You don't know what that means?"

"No," said Pappy, "I don't. What's it mean?"

Tom felt the frustration welling up from his soul. "I don't know either! I'm just looking for anything that will help us."

"I think that is Chinese."

"It would be really nice if you had brought your loan agreement. That was the whole purpose of this meeting."

"I did bring it," said Pappy.

Tom crossed his arms and waited while his father reached into first one pocket, then a second, then a third.

Pappy mumbled to himself. "It was in here somewheres. Ah, there."

He produced a rolled-up sheaf of papers that looked like it'd been used to swat flies for years. It was stained with brown splotches and unrecognizable bits of hardened gunk.

"Dusty had ta dig it up from somewheres in the office," he explained. "He found it under the coffee pot. We haven't really looked at it fer years."

Tom gingerly accepted the document, wishing that he'd brought surgical gloves and a pair of tongs. Nonetheless, he unrolled the paperwork and set the water glasses on the corners of the papers and began to read the agreement.

"This is barely legible, Pappy."

"I know it," he said sadly. "Dusty used 'em ta paper over the windows fer a few years 'fore he realized his mistake."

Tom squinted and tried to decipher the same paragraph in his father's contract. "It looks like you have the same window."

"What does that mean?"

"That it's boilerplate language. We probably won't get anywhere with it."

He sat back and sighed. At that moment, Madge arrived with their order. "Hi, boys. One oatmeal special for Tom, and . . . another order of bacon with a side of pickles for Pappy."

She stood back. "Everything good?"

"You betcha," said Pappy.

Madge glanced at their documents. "Those look like loan agreements from the bank."

"They are," said Tom, amazed at her acuity.

"Withers got you two over a barrel or somethin'?"

"More like in a barrel, rollin' down a hill," said Pappy, "and it's all revenge fer me stealin' a girl from him when we was young."

"Which girl?" she said.

Pappy nodded toward Tom. "That one's mother. She's not here anymore, I'm sure ya know, but boy was she a purty one. I never told her that. Maybe I oughta have." He regretfully scratched at his long, gnarly, thinning hair that was still left on his scalp.

"She was fortunate to have a man like yourself to keep her happy," beamed Madge, "happier than Withers would've."

Tom grew suddenly interested. "You have any dirt on him?"

She swelled with pride. "I got enough dirt to bury an army, sweetheart. J. Edgar Hoover used to call *me* lookin' for information."

She nudged Tom with her arm. He grinned at her, not knowing how else to reply.

Madge continued: "Well, one a his goons is kinda sweet on me, and he comes in here last week tellin' me how everybody's upset because somebody is stealin' money from the customers of the bank. I ask who, and he just points upstairs. I said, God? He said, almost. I said, Withers? His lips wouldn't say, but his look sure did."

"Withers is stealing money from people?"

"So there you have it. That's all I got. Lemme know if you need anything else." Madge punctuated the end of the gossip with the swift nod of a head, and then she was gone.

Without hesitation, Tom rolled up their loan agreements. "Forget the nit-picking over language, Pappy. That is how we get Withers."

"How do we prove *that?*"

Tom's eyes were lit with passion. "We'll find a way."

"But Madge could be—"

Tom guessed what his father was going to say. "Madge is never wrong, you can swear by that. She's the grease that makes this town run." He caught his father's eyes. "God willing, Withers's days as the head of that bank are numbered."

Chapter 19

"Tubby, we can do this later," said Tom, waiting, his hands impatiently on his hips. "I've got a lot going on right now."

They were standing on the tarmac. Tom was facing the farm crop duster, and his pilot was chest deep in the guts of the vehicle's engine, his head and arms and shoulders totally gone from view.

"No, no, I've almost got it," Tubby's voice said. "Something is gunking up the compressor. Oh, hey! Got it! That was easy!"

Tubby closed the hatch to the crop duster's engine, pulled the stepladder up to the side of the plane, and gestured to the back seat. "The boss goes first, sir."

Taking a deep breath, Tom mounted the stepladder and hoisted himself into the back of the crop duster. He always felt like he was taking his life into his hands by flying with Tubby. Strapped beneath the plane were two large tanks of a new bug spray. It'd cost Tom a pretty penny from the agricultural supply company, money that he didn't have. He had to make one last ditch effort to save his farm from foreclosure, ultimate destruction, and failure. He had to find a way to bring the investors back and eliminate Withers's threat.

Tubby started the motor and spun the propeller, then hopped in behind the stick. He pulled back, and the crop duster rolled down the dirt tarmac and lifted into the air. Tom felt his stomach rise up to his throat. It always did that in these tiny planes. It was like driving a Porsche—you felt every bump in the air.

Tubby circled around to the far end of the fields and dove down to less than twenty meters above the stalks. Tom felt something fall out of his pocket as they went down. He tried to look to see what it was and where it went but became disoriented in the fall. He finally saw something somewhat brown floating somewhere between the plane and the ground. He suddenly remembered he had kept putting the chili package in his pocket, not quite sure the direction he wanted to take with the whole chili/Mine Moppet fiasco. He dismissed the package as temporarily lost. Tubby leveled out and began to systematically pass across the corn, the plane spewing clouds of bug killer. In the backseat, Tom worked the tanks, opening the gates when they needed it, closing the gates when they lifted up to circle around.

"Everything OK back there?" shouted Tubby.

"Perfect," said Tom. "If this works!"

Below, in the field . . .

The package of Pappy's Chilly Mountain Chili Mix fluttered down through the air and landed in the thick soil of the field. It came to rest against one of the massive Ubercorn stalks.

Lacey, the Skeletonizer Beetle waddled over, hard hat and gas mask on. Lacey considered the chili, how strangely it had fallen from the sky, then figured it was meant to be. She grabbed and dragged it off.

Lacey pulled the package up to a pile of other packages. Once the dust settled from the insecticide, she began opening the packages she had found, thanks to Bojangles handiwork and Mary Ann's perseverance.

She had flown into the granary when the smell wafted out, while Mary Ann was busily counting the packages. She knew this powder. Mary Ann had counted and, in her haste, had left the door to the little room wide open. This was the perfect opportunity for this little beetle to pursue the glorious smell permeating from the room. She had entered and had just started to get a good whiff when she had begun to get extremely dizzy. This had been confusing to her. It shouldn't be this way. Stunned, she had sluggishly found her way out as though she had been drugged. Once far enough out, she had begun to breathe fresh, clean air. There was something about that substance.

After a few minutes of drinking in the fresh air, her tiny brain had begun working clearly. What had just happened? Suddenly, it had occurred to her. It was as if the substance which had given her new life was working against her. The realization had hit her.

She had been just like any other Skeletonizer Beetle. Then she had become lost one day while burrowing in the ground and had found herself in a place so magical and joyful. She had stayed, finding a new family.

One day, as she was busy burrowing, which was her favorite pastime, she had surfaced back upside. She was in a strange, yet beautiful aromatic place. Suddenly, a giant figure had appeared. It had caught her by surprise. It had leaned in close. Somehow it hadn't seemed threatening. She remembered looking at this strange figure, and it spoke. Strange as it seemed, she had understood. She had tried to respond vocally, but all she could make come out was squeaking. The only way she could think of to communicate was through actions. Soon, she had gone back to her new home and had found out he was a human and a boy. They had quickly become friends.

One morning, bright and early, she had seen something strange. There were more humans, not the usual ones who were there often, in the fields. They had been carrying giant pails, similar to what she had seen at her new home below the surface, and they had reached in and had pulled out creatures which looked just like herself. At first, she had been excited. She had tried to communicate with her likeness, but they had not understood. Soon, she had seen them begin to eat and to destroy the beautiful land she was in. This had hurt her. This was her new friend's home too. She did not like this at all.

Now she must do something and, after her experience in the strange room, had thought of just the right idea. She had felt she needed to get back there. But how? It had occurred to her to go back to her new home and find out what she could do. She had soon found the location she had entered into this beautiful place and had reentered it following the path back to her new home. She had been supplied with needed items and had returned to face the new and dangerous challenge to save her newfound friend's home.

As she looked back upon her experiences, she poured out the contents and then used a tiny shovel to scoop out some chili and fill a tiny patchwork canvas bag with the maroon powder. Then the Skeletonizer Beetle, small as she was, started shuffling along the corn rows, spreading the chili powder, similar to a farmer spreading seed. Suddenly, an ugly little worm appeared before her. Lacey filled her palm with chili and blew the dust into the worm's face. The worm first displayed confusion then gathered its wits and quickly squirmed away.

Chapter 20

Tom stood behind Pappy in front of the bathroom mirror, teaching his father how to tie a necktie. His hands were on top of his father's hands, guiding them.

"Up and over," Tom said, "then around like this, no, not there, yes, there. Good. Now cinch it tight."

With a swift move, Pappy yanked the tie so hard on his neck that he started to choke. Tom loosened it for him. "Easy does it, Pappy. I think we're ready."

They stepped out of Tom's house and climbed into his truck. The trip into the business district of town took about twenty minutes, and neither of them said much. The brick building rolled up on the left, a lonely but strong, independent structure.

The bank examiner.

A species of auditor, a bank examiner served as an extension of the state government, and they acted to evaluate institutional compliance with relevant regulations and laws. This meant that they made sure the banks followed the rules, particularly in record-keeping, data entry, and transaction regulations.

This was a long shot, but talking to this man was the only hope Tom and Pappy had left, at least for the moment.

Tom parked the truck, and he and Pappy walked up to the front door and rang the office doorbell. He looked down at his father's shoes. They were caked with dirt. "Couldn't you have shined your shoes, Pappy?"

"Nope," replied Pappy. "I feel more honest like this."

"It's a sign of respect."

Pappy shrugged. "Well, I don't know if'n I respect 'em yet."

A secretary opened the door, welcomed them inside, took their coats, offered them some coffee or tea, and then led them toward a door with a sign that read *Sam Wolfe, Bank Examiner.*

"Excuse me, but I thought we were supposed to be meeting with an Arye Buck," said Tom.

"Mr. Buck no longer works in this office," said the secretary. "He left the position yesterday."

"Where did he go?"

The secretary leveled a glance at him. "To go work for the bank as a director."

Tom barely had time to react to that before he found himself shaking hands with Sam Wolfe. Wolfe was a towering, intense man with a habit of peering at everybody over the tops of his glasses as though the world were full of dead specimens pinned to display boards.

"Mr. Powers, Mr. Powers," he said, "Sam Wolfe." He pumped both Tom's and Pappy's hands vigorously. "Thank you for coming, and please have a seat."

The visitors settled themselves in the two guest chairs, while the bank examiner returned to the other side of the desk. He settled himself in the captain's seat, put his elbows on the chair arms, steepled his fingers, and said, "What can I help you with today?"

"We have a concern about the Mighty Bank of Elites," said Tom.

"And that concern is . . ."

Before Tom could reply, Pappy cut in. "We think Mr. Withers is robbin' his own bank blind," then added, "Sir."

That took Sam Wolfe by surprise. "That's a tall accusation. What have you got to back it up?"

"Well," replied Tom, hemming a little, "it's interesting you ask that because we thought you might investigate."

The man seemed taken aback. "You think that you can just walk in here off the streets and ask me to investigate on just a thought?"

"It'd be awfully nice a ye," said Pappy.

Tom waved his father off. "We are friends with Madge." He waited for the importance of that remark to sink in.

It didn't. Sam Wolfe shrugged at the insinuation of power. "Everybody knows Madge. She owns a diner. So what?"

"And she told us that one of Withers's goons said that he's been stealing money from the consumers of the bank."

"Is that so?" asked the bank examiner, clearly unimpressed.

"Yes. So we'd like to know what can be done about this."

Sam studied his fingers. "You mean to tell me that all you have is *gossip*?"

"Isn't that where most investigations begin?" said Tom. "We're bringing you a valuable tip."

Sam Wolfe unsteepled his fingers and leaned forward. "I'm not going to investigate the Mighty Bank of Elites because two yokels who can't pay their bills heard something from somebody who said that a goon said something. That's ludicrous. What made you think that I would help you?"

"Desperation," said Pappy, then added, pointing at Tom, "and I ain't behind on my bill, just him. I pay my bill just fine."

Wolfe grimaced. He stood up and gestured to the door. "I need you guys out of my office. I can't go accusing one of our most powerful bank executives around these parts of stealing based upon diner gossip. Frankly, this looks like a cheap attempt on the part of you men to get out of paying your debts, well at least one of you." Then focusing his attention on Pappy, he continued, "I understand you may want to help your son, being very noble and all, but you came here with nothing. If you want anything done, you need to do it the right way. Now good day to you!"

Pappy jumped up and retorted, "Now wait ya just a minute here. I did not come here just ta be turned away. I tell ya we know from experience Withers is crooked in a bad way. He even threatened my son here. He's even tryin' ta have me considered looney so he can take my mine. Now my son here has nothin' ta do with that, and he may be behind on a few payments, but I think that Withers is tryin' ta get our properties ta make a profit. My son here has 'bout a thousand acres a land full a nice giant rainbow corn. That'd be a nice profit fer a man ta get ahold of. And my mine has a special substance I'm sure he'd like ta get ta. Ya may not care 'bout us none, but there's others what say he's stealin'. That should count fer somethin.'"

Tom sat listening to his father's speech in amazement. He had just made the sanest comments Tom had heard in a very long time. He supposed Pappy had his moments, but he was shocked nonetheless. After hearing his father make his speech, Tom stood, and he began to push Pappy toward the door.

Pappy stopped at the door and said, "Thank ya fer yer time."

Sam Wolfe looked at him a moment, and his sour face softened. "Let me know if you find something concrete, and give me a written request for investigation, eh?"

Tom pulled Pappy out of the office, and they headed back to the truck. Once inside, Tom thumped his head against the steering wheel and exhaled. "Well, that's probably it for us, Pappy. Thank you for standing up for me, though, even if you did throw me under the bus a little bit."

"Naw, ya heard what he said. We got's ta give 'im some concrete and put our request in writin'. I'm sure we'll make it somehow. And I am not 'bout ta throw ya under a bus. That would be a very bad thang," said Pappy.

Chapter 21

At the entrance to Pappy's mine, Tom crouched in front of Jimmy, trying to find a way to fit an adult-sized hardhat onto Jimmy's little head.

"It's too big," his son complained.

"Let me adjust it, hang on."

Tom stepped back and admired his son. The hat was secure, but it hung all the way over the boy's face. He had to lift his head upward just to see his father. "Perfect," said Tom.

"Daddy, why are we here?"

"We're going to see your grandpa's mine. You can count it like a field trip. It's educational."

Pappy approached with another hard hat, which he handed to Tom. "Hoo boy, the Mine Moppets'r gonna be excited ta see this little fella."

"Daddy," Jimmy asked, "are we gonna see those the little guys Pappy was talking about?"

"No, son, I just thought we might check out the place where your grandfather has been hanging his hat for all these years. These magical creatures are just in his head son."

"Then why does Pappy keep talking about them?"

"Cause he's out of his ever-loving—"

"I don't hafta talk 'bout 'em. They'll take care a that themselves." Pappy turned to Dusty. "Want ta give 'em a quick tour a the mine?"

"Course," Dusty replied. He pulled aside the fence that protected the entrance to the mine. They stepped inside. Then he pulled aside a gated door revealing a tiny, rickety elevator car, a single light bulb hanging above the cage. The three men and the boy crammed themselves inside and Dusty closed the gate and pulled a handle, and the elevator started to descend.

After a minute of descent into the darkness, Tom started to sweat. He wondered if bringing Jimmy on this little tour had been a good idea. The elevator picked up speed, and finally, they arrived at the base of the mine with a jolt so hard it hurt Tom's knees. Dusty opened the gate, and they stepped out into a tunnel lined with all different shades of purple covering the walls.

"What is that?" said Jimmy.

"Pappy's salt," said Tom.

"That's *rainbow* salt," said Pappy. "This's the purple vein. We've got all differ'nt varieties down here."

Jimmy pulled off a loose piece of salt and stared at it. The wall reformed and filled in the gap where he'd been.

"Look't that," said Pappy.

He was pointing to the place in the wall where Jimmy had pulled off the piece. The purple walls had filled in the small gap.

"Wow!" said Jimmy.

"This's a special mine," said Pappy. "Now ya can go ahead and put that in your mouth, but ya might regret it."

Jimmy put the salt into his mouth, then immediately spat it out at his feet and made a disgusted face. "It's gross!"

Dusty and Pappy laughed.

"Purple ain't no good on its own, young'un," said Dusty. "We grind it up an' mix it with the other varieties."

"Blecch!" Jimmy shouted, running his fingers inside his mouth.

"Careful now," Pappy said. "The Mine Moppets don't like loud voices."

Jimmy froze. If there was any chance he might see one, Tom knew Jimmy wasn't going to miss it. Tom wondered how many years he'd bought into such foolishness. How long had he believed? This endeavor would crush Jimmy's spirit when they returned to the surface without a Mine Moppet sighting. Tom wished he'd thought of that earlier; he wanted Jimmy to be young at heart as long as possible.

"I built these tunnels by hand," said Pappy, dragging his fingertips over the wall. "Twenty years a diggin'."

"You could've asked for help," said Tom.

"I wouldn't've asked ya ta sacrifice so much."

"You didn't ask me if you could go away either, so what did it matter?"

Dusty led Jimmy through the tunnels, pointing out the empty mine carts that were used to carry out the salt. He even hoisted the boy into one.

"Careful, son, Pappy's going to turn you into chili," said Tom.

"That would be awesome!"

Dusty lifted him out, and they continued walking. A minute later, the tunnel dead-ended at a wooden door. Jimmy tried to find a way to open it, running his hands all over the smooth wood. "Pappy, there's no handle," he said.

"Ya have ta knock an' then wait fer the Mine Moppets ta open the door," Dusty said.

Frustrated, Tom elbowed Dusty. "Why are you playing into this nonsense? My son believes you."

The mine manager looked at him with clear eyes. "It ain't nonsense."

"Have you ever even seen one of these so-called Magical Mine Moppets?"

"Ya betcha, I have, lotsa times."

Tom just shook his head. He was surrounded by nut jobs.

Jimmy banged on the door and stepped back and waited. Everything fell into silence in the mine, except for the sound of the men and boy breathing. They waited about five minutes.

"I guess they're in the middle of a meetin'," said Pappy finally. "Maybe next time."

Jimmy looked sad, so Tom kneeled in front of him. "Cheer up, son. Pappy's got quite an imagination, doesn't he?"

"Yeah, I guess so," Jimmy dejectedly responded.

"They're all just stories, son."

Then Jimmy shrieked and pointed over Tom's shoulder. "I just saw one! He has on a cowboy hat!"

"Aw! He's a sneaky one, that cowboy," Pappy said. "Won't do no good, though. That thar is Sam S. Cowboy. He won't help us none."

Tom whirled around, scanning the darkness. Nothing. Of course. "Pappy, there's nothing there. That's just the power of suggestion, son."

"The what?"

"It means we get told something and then we want to believe it so bad we make it happen."

"Oh," Jimmy responded, "OK. I guess it's just like Lacey. I want so much to see her doing things, but it's all just my imagination?"

"Something like that, but you're just a kid, and it's normal to pretend things. Pappy here is a grown-up, and when you grow up, you have to put away your child fantasies and be in reality. Pappy just told himself for so long that these Mine Moppet creatures were real, he started believing they were. I am not saying you have to get rid of your imagination, that's what makes the world tick. I just want you to understand that we grow up and have to do grown-up things. Now stop telling this boy lies, Pappy."

"I'm not lyin', but someday you'll know it," said Pappy.

"I'm ready to go now. This is useless. You own this mine, and we can't even get in it. You had better not be up to something."

"I ain't up ta nothin'."

"Exactly. There's nothing to see here. I don't even know why I wasted our time coming here. I'm done. Let's go."

The men walked the boy back to the elevator.

Tom felt stupid. Maybe he shouldn't have subjected Jimmy to all this.

Chapter 22

As Sam Wolfe arrived at the top floor of the Mighty Bank of Elites, he only had eyes for the door at the other end of the room. To the bank examiner, there was only one person worth speaking to on this floor—the big kahuna, Mr. Withers.

A few days earlier, after Pappy and Tom had unceremoniously left his office, he had leaned back in his chair and thought about their complaint. The comment by one of Withers's goons to Madge was a good tip, though he hadn't wanted to tell them that. It also wasn't the only tip that he'd received. In fact, he had an entire drawer full of comments from people wondering about the shady things that went on inside the bank. The prior examiner had to have been covering up. Maybe he had been paid off. Maybe that was why he went to the bank as the new director. He could shift the numbers and keep up the farce. Or maybe he was brought in to fix it before the bank went under. Whatever the case, he had left evidence behind. It looked like someone in that bank was cheating the system. Most of the complaints came in from prior loan customers.

The next morning, he'd decided to do something about that.

It'd taken a few days of concentrated analysis, a few days of reports studied, of requests made and ignored—but eventually, he found that things just didn't look right. It seemed, in a preliminary study of the paperwork, that Withers might have indeed been soaking money for personal use from the Mighty Bank of Elites through the insider loan process. He had seen the repeated loans Withers had with the bank. They were under the limits, but people had complained to his office that the bank had foreclosed on their properties and then devalued them. Many of the loans Withers had taken out he saw were ones that had been devalued foreclosure properties that had gone to auction. Withers had personally won the auctions and took out loans to pay for them. Wolfe had now found possible proof, and maybe he was wrong, but he was duty-bound to report, in person, that people were pointing fingers at Withers.

He walked down the row of secretaries, ignoring their calls and questions. He'd been through this many times before at other companies, and he'd found that it was in his best interest to appear disinterested. That meant ignoring everything that everybody said to him, as though he were a ghost.

He knocked on Withers's office door, the secretaries having stood up and followed behind him. The door swung open a minute later, and the sharp beak of the bank president stood there. Several tiny daubs of toilet paper were stuck to his face.

"What is it?"

"Mr. Withers, Sam Wolfe, bank examiner."

Withers practically spat on the floor. "Oh, did one of my employees forget to tie their shoe this morning?"

Said Wolfe, "It's a tad more serious than that. May I come in?"

Withers waved him inside, then waved off the secretaries, who buzzed back to their desks. He closed the door behind Wolfe.

They took their places on opposite sides of his desk. The air in the room was doubly stuffy. Wolfe put his briefcase on his lap and folded his hands gently on top. Withers sat down behind the desk with his hands folded behind his head. Rings of sweat appeared under his armpits. He seemed nervous, thought Wolfe.

"Well, out with it," said Withers.

Wolfe cleared his throat. "This is a formal announcement that my office has decided to move forward with an investigation of your bank. Specifically, of your activities within the bank."

"You've waited a long time," said Withers. "I've been expecting this for years."

"Why is that?" said Wolfe.

"Because the higher the monkey climbs in the tree, the more of his hiney there is to see."

"Very poetic," replied the bank examiner. "Would you like to hear more?"

"No, but I'll listen."

Wolfe outlined his concerns—the contradictory numbers that he found in the paperwork, the possible discrepancy between what the bank had claimed in loan agreements with consumers and the subsequent foreclosures, the auctions the bank had, and how somehow the properties were devalued at less than their actual worth. He didn't mention Withers by name. He just watched and waited for his response.

"Surely you can't expect me to extend forgiveness to all of my delinquent loans."

Wolfe glanced at the paperwork. "Nearly seventy-two percent of your debtors defaulted on their loans last year."

"It's been a difficult economy."

"The national average is about twenty-six percent."

"We're poor here," he said. "It's an agricultural area, no rain. I don't know. I'm not a weatherman. I'm not a priest or a minister. I'm just a transactional person. I make deals and execute the terms of the deal."

Wolfe listened to him go on for a while. They usually did, the presidents, take his investigation very personally. It didn't always mean that they were guilty of wrongdoing, but he had a feeling in this instance that Withers was hiding some bad stuff. And that would mean that Withers was both crooked and intelligent, a terrible combination. It was easier when criminals were stupid.

"Do you have any proof?" said Withers.

"We have suggestions and complaints of improprieties, and I've taken a look at prior loan records and other related bank business."

"That's not proof of foul play."

"No, but I'd still like to investigate."

Withers grew cold. "Then my staff will assist in any way that they can."

Sam Wolfe rose, pushed in his chair, and began to leave the office. Then he stopped in the doorway. "And one more thing—if I do uncover your personal involvement in any of these improprieties, you lose personally. Just to be clear."

Withers sat there, frozen. The bank examiner left the room and shut the door. He watched the door close. When it had clicked, he exhaled. "OK," he said.

Young Lin came tumbling out of the closet, his mouth full, wiping his fingers on his pants. He'd been eating in there.

"Yes sir," he said. A piece of chewed bread flew out of his mouth, sailed across the desk, and struck Withers on the shoulder. It stayed there, to Young Lin's consternation.

Withers didn't say anything for the longest while. Young Lin stood there, sweating, unable to take his eyes off the spitty morsel. At last, Withers said, "We need to secure that Powers farm, and we need Pappy's mine, and I mean now, boy! Otherwise, we'll soon be living in cardboard boxes."

Chapter 23

In the mine office later that day, Dusty settled in his chair, feet up and the tiny television blaring. He heard the screeching of tires on gravel.

"Hey Pappy," he shouted, "ya ferget somethin'?"

There was no response, so he went to the window. Outside stood a shiny black SUV, and two people he didn't know—one angular and hawk-like, the other young and deferential.

"We didn't forget anything, Dusty," one of the strangers called out. "Come on out and let's talk for a minute."

Dusty hitched up his overalls, turned off the television, then warily walked outside. "Whatchu want?" he cautiously asked.

"My name is Withers, and this is my associate, Young Lin."

A light dawned inside Dusty's cranium. He'd heard these names before. "Ah no. Yu'uns from that thar bank, hain't ya?"

"I am. And I'm here to make you an offer, Dusty."

Dusty really had no intention of paying them any mind, but company was company when you lived in the boonies. "Whelp, maybe I can hear ya out, but I gotsta get sompin' first." He held up a finger and disappeared into the shack.

Withers and Young Lin looked at each other, confused.

Dusty returned with his favorite stuffed chair and set it up on the dirt. He pointed to his head. "My thinkin' chair. I cain't figger nuttin 'thout it." He plopped back into the chair. "A'right. I'll hear ya out."

Withers proceeded. "Dusty, you're in a losing battle, and I'm here to invite you to join the winners' side."

"That so?" he asked, picking food out of his teeth.

"Yes." Withers launched into some jargon that left Dusty bored.

Dusty let out an exaggerated sigh and began to toss a ball in the air.

Young Lin nudged his boss and whispered, "Sir, could I suggest using smaller words." Withers paused then continued. "Dusty, I'm going to—"

"I'm gonna—" whispered Young Lin, again.

Withers corrected himself: "—I'm *gonna* take this mine away from Pappy."

"Sez you'uns. Pappy owns this here mine."

"We're bringing him to a mental competency hearing next week. When that hearing is concluded, ownership of the mine will be shifted over to me and my bank, permanently. Why I'm here, is for your help."

Dusty stuck out his chin stubbornly. "Not me. I'm loyal ta Pappy."

"Admirable. But you understand that once I'm finished, Pappy will be left with nothing, which means you will be left with nothing. No mine, no job, no money. It's my side or nothing."

"Well, Pappy'll take care a me."

"Pappy won't have squat either. Nope. You will be out in the cold, Dusty, old boy. I will win. With your help or without. But I would like to help you if you help me."

Dusty looked concerned now. He leaned forward and responded. "So I'ma gonna tell ya what I'ma thinkin'. I ain't sayin' I'ma gonna help, but . . . whoncha tell me what I gots ta do."

Withers stepped forward, close to Dusty, smelled him, and stepped back as the odor overcame him. It was as if he hadn't taken a bath in months. He composed himself, smiled reluctantly, and responded. "Just testify and tell the court exactly what Pappy tells you about the Magical Mine Moppets."

"That's it?"

"Yes."

"I ain't gots ta lie?"

"No."

"And what da I git?"

"I'll make you manager of this mine."

Dusty retorted, "I'm a'ready manager."

"You won't be when Pappy loses it! But, now, you help me, and you'll be manager forever, Dusty. Forever and ever." Withers then upped the ante. "I'll even give you a raise."

Dusty raised his eyebrows. "You'uns buy me a truck too?" The words just came tumbling out like they weren't his. "Ya give me a big'un, with the fancy wheels and the disc player. The one what holds six, not just the one; the six." He held up six coarse fingers.

"You'll get it all," said Withers. "Now do we have a deal?"

Withers stretched out his hand. Dusty looked at it, then stood up and grasped Withers's hand and pumped it twice, making the bank president gasp from the power and strength. Afterward, Young Lin handed Withers a handkerchief. He discreetly wiped his hand.

"We'll see you in court next Thursday at ten a.m. You know how to get to town?"

"I been there once."

"We'll pick you up."

A moment later, Young Lin and Withers turned and walked back to the black vehicle. The assistant opened the door, let the banker in, and followed him inside.way.

Once securely inside, Young Lin stated quietly, "the hearing is at one p.m. sir."

"I know," Withers responded. "Send a car for him at nine."

"Yes, sir."

Withers looked out the window at Dusty, who had sat back down and was lolling around in his chair, and stated to himself, "Pappy, you've made your last move—and it's checkmate."

Dusty watched attentively as the fancy vehicle pulled away. Soon the sound of the engine and tires pulling against the gravel disappeared, and all that was left was the whistling of the desert wind. For a moment, Dusty felt regret. He wanted to change his mind. Then he looked around at his little cabin. This was home. If Pappy couldn't keep him here, then Withers would, and he couldn't help Pappy keep the mine. Would've if he could've but he couldn't.

He took his treasured thinkin' chair back inside and sat down, no longer feeling like thinking. He leaned forward and clicked the television back on and soon all the troubles were gone from his mind.

Chapter 24

Tom sat in a booth at Madge's Diner, paperwork strewn before him. He sensed a coffee pot arrive, and his mug was refilled.

He looked up. Madge's smiling face looked down at him. "Baby," she said, "I got some news for you."

Tom's ears perked up. "What is it?"

"I heard that Withers is goin' after your Pappy's mine. Gonna do whatever it takes. His goon told me that he's going to have the state declare Pappy mentally incompetent. There's going to be a hearing. Not sure when. I didn't have time to find out more. All I know is he is on the warpath. He just keeps babbling on about Pappy, his mine, and your farm."

Tom held himself stock still. He already knew Withers was after their properties. He didn't understand why Withers wanted them so much. The jealousy was over, wasn't it? He hoped Withers would not do something dangerous or threatening. Madge was almost never wrong, and he had disregarded this at his peril.

He managed to choke out a thank you. She laid a friendly hand on his shoulder and patted him before moving along to the next booth.

Tom felt the panic starting to rise in his body. He had to find a way out of this. As soon as Pappy started talking about the Mine Moppets, it was over.

There was only one thing left to do.

He gathered his paperwork, left a few dollars on the table, and raced home to his wife and warn her that Withers could become destructive.

That Friday night, Tom entered Salt Slab Steakhouse dressed in his best suit. It was his second visit, and he had nothing left to lose.

The hostess greeted him with a big smile. "Hello, do you have a reservation?"

Tom scanned the restaurant over her shoulder. There, in the corner, the same table as before, sat Withers. Opposite him was another woman.

"No," he replied, "I'm meeting somebody."

Drawing a deep breath, he moved through the tables toward the bank president. Withers looked up and saw him approach, and a steely look appeared on his face.

"Mr. Withers," Tom said, offering a firm handshake, "It's such a surprise to see you here!"

The bank president's face was made of ice. "I'm sure it is."

"Listen, my wife isn't going to get here for a few minutes, so I'm going to join you guys. Don't worry, I'll be gone before you know it." Without waiting for a reply, Tom pulled a chair out from beneath a woman at a nearby table. She fell on the floor.

Tom settled himself at the side of the table, lifted a finger to a passing waiter and said, "I'll take an orange soda."

"It's a steakhouse."

"Don't try to water it down either, my friend." He made an I'm-watching-you gesture with two fingers, and the waiter went away.

Withers's date's mouth had literally dropped open. "Hi, Jessica," said Tom.

"My name is Jolene," she said.

"Well, I had the first letter right."

They shook hands, and Tom turned to Withers and rapped on the menu. "What kinda slop are they serving here tonight, Withers? Forty-two varieties of bloody cow?"

A burst of laughter escaped Jolene's mouth. Then she quickly covered her mouth with a hand.

Withers wasn't amused. "What do you want, Powers?"

"First I want to show you how easy it is to get a woman authentically interested in you." He turned to Jolene. "Right, Jessica?"

"Jolene."

"Hey, gimme a break. It's not easy to crash a table like this."

She smiled in spite of herself. "Yes, you're attractive, Tom."

"Does it have anything to do with how I look?"

"Not really."

"Or how much money I have?"

She shrugged. "I don't know how much money you have."

Withers spoke up. "Tom here doesn't have two nickels to rub together. In fact, he owes me."

Tom drew in a deep breath. "And that's why I'm here, Withers. If you drop the mental competency hearing against my father, I am willing to give you my farm with no contest."

Withers looked at him. "That's very noble, Tom."

"He is my father, Mr. Withers. Human relationships are important, you know."

Jolene looked at Withers expectantly. Tom knew it was good to have this little bit of sympathy from a woman that he was trying to impress.

Withers thought about it. "That's fair. I'll have the papers sent over on Monday. You'll have to vacate immediately."

Tom rose, bowed solemnly to the lady, and left the table, passing the waiter who was arriving with his orange soda.

He kept his head high and his brave front intact until he arrived at his truck in the parking lot. He shut the door behind him, thumped his head against the steering wheel, and started to cry.

Tom Powers had just lost his farm, the family farm.

Chapter 25

The pen scratched on the signature line, and a second later Tom handed the document over.

He was at his kitchen table. Sitting next to him was Mary Anne, tears in her eyes, handkerchief in her hands. Her arm was around Jimmy, who watched the proceedings with scared eyes.

Standing over the family were Withers's goons, and next to them was Young Lin. The assistant looked through the document, checking that everything had been filled out properly.

"Once this is filed," said Young Lin, "your property will be repossessed by the bank. You will have to vacate immediately after."

Mary Anne watched him, her lips pursed into a small rictus of anger. "How do you live with yourself?"

"I don't have to," said the assistant, putting the papers in his briefcase. "Mr. Withers owns my life."

Tom stood up, pain in his expression, yet calmness in his voice, as he said, "You can take everything here, Young Lin. It doesn't matter. I'll be back and bigger than ever." He put his hand out to his son. "Let's go, Jimmy."

At one point in time, Tom's truck had been so new and shiny that it looked slick and almost wet under the sun. But now, as it rolled through the weeping Ubercorn, the car looked as dull as the dying stalks. The dusty wheels spun over the gravel with a rolling *crunch*, the only sound for miles.

None of this was going to be his, not anymore. The thought depressed Tom so much that he focused on his driving instead.

Jimmy rode shotgun, quiet as midnight until he abruptly let out a strange noise. "*Rawwwrp!*"

Tom looked at him with a crinkled forehead. "Jimmy! What was that?""

Pappy said I have to practice my *rawrp*."

"But why? What is it?"

"It's the sound that the Mine Moppets make."

Tom bit his lip, started to correct the boy, and then stopped himself. At this moment, he didn't have it in him to start another fight. It wasn't worth the effort.

"Really."

"Pappy says if it's not perfect, like exactly right, the Mine Moppets won't come. He said you wouldn't believe me when I said it."

"Pappy knows me well."

"*Rawwwwrp!*"

Tom sighed.

They arrived at the mine, and the door to the office shack flew open. Dusty stumbled out, catching himself from tripping over the one and only step, dust caked over every last inch of his coveralls. "Heya Tommy. Yer pappy, he, uh . . ." Here he paused, not for dramatic effect, but because the world was moving too fast for him. "He's a'ready gone down."

"Rawwwwwrp!" Jimmy couldn't help himself.

The sound made Dusty stop like he'd just walked into a glass sliding door—his arms wind-milling backward at the shock, landing his behind in the dirt. He shook his head as if to awaken himself from a dream.

"He's been practicing," Tom said, extending a helpful hand to Dusty.

He popped up with no attempt to brush off the new dirt he'd acquired. "Wooee! Think that'll draw the whole colony of 'em." He scratched Jimmy's mop of hair and waved for them to follow him to the elevator shaft. The industrial door opened and closed behind them, the small container lowering them deep into the ground.

"Rawwwrp! Rawwwrp! Rawwwrp!" Jimmy's expression was eager with anticipation after each call.

"So when do we actually mine this, uh, rainbow salt?" Tom said.

"Hopefully today, if the Mine Moppets let us. They call the shots 'round here."

Not only was Tom done arguing about the existence of Magical Mine Moppets, but he knew better than to do so with a guy like Dusty, who was a few cards short of a deck. How had Pappy convinced him to believe in these Mine Moppets? The two of them spoke of the Mine Moppets in the same way, like they'd just seen them a few minutes earlier. Tom secretly wished he could have been coaxed to believe in them; it might have made growing up easier.

They stepped out of the elevator and moved through the tunnel of purple salt. Tom rapped on the walls with his knuckles.

"So how do we get started?"

"Pappy wants ta introduce you'uns ta the Mine Moppets first," said Dusty.

They arrived at the wooden door that they had seen a few days before. It was ajar, so Dusty leaned in with an ear.

"Sounds like Pappy's a'ready talkin' wit' 'em," he whispered. He turned to Jimmy: "Who wantsta go first?"

"Meeeee!" Jimmy said. He ran to the door and used all his might to open it beyond a little crack. "It's heavy!"

Tom stepped up, "Careful son," and helped pull the door open wide. Whatever they were expecting, it wasn't on the other side. The three stared down a long tunnel featuring rainbow-colored salts—deep reds, oranges, yellows, greens, blues, indigos, and purples. Jimmy took off running.

"No running in the rainbow tunnel!" Tom shouted.

"Rawwwwrp!" he shouted, still going full speed ahead.

Tom decided to let him run. He turned to the mine manager. "Dusty, what's really down here?"

"The Magical Mine Moppets." Dusty took a toothpick out of his pocket and shoved it between his teeth.

"No, really."

"Ya hear all right? I a'ready told ya."

Tom was itching for an adult conversation but was clearly barking up the wrong nut tree.

They crept slowly through the dim tunnel, Tom out of hesitation and Dusty because slow was the only speed he knew. Far ahead, Tom heard his son's *rawwrps*. He turned on the flashlight from his cell phone and waved it from side to side, scanning the tunnel. Nothing.

"Look, thar's a Mine Moppet right yonder," said Dusty. He pointed with his toothpick.

Tom swung the light over to the area but saw nothing. "Yeah, right."

Dusty shrugged. "He got himself scared, ran off. Ya wansta keep goin'?"

"I have to," said Tom, rolling his eyes. This whole thing was crazy, and Tom was going to get to the bottom of it, *that day*. He had spent his entire life enduring such shenanigans, and now he'd put a stop to the madness. Besides, he wasn't in the mood. He had just lost his farm, and they had a lot of salt to mine, although he knew that they could never scratch out a living from a salt mine.

Jimmy came streaking back to them from out of the darkness. "Daddy, there's a whole town of Mine Moppets in there!" The skepticism must've registered on Tom's face because Jimmy tugged at his daddy's sleeve. "No, seriously! You have to see!"

"Got me an idea," Dusty said. "Jimmy, let's say we puts a blindfold on you'uns daddy ta take him in. Mine Moppets'll think that's a hoot." He let out a goofy laugh and pulled a sweaty bandana from his back pocket and presented it to Tom.

"Yeah! Daddy, put it on!"

He put up a token resistance, then relented and allowed Dusty to put on the dirty blindfold.

"Just to humor Jimmy," he said.

"Let's go!" Jimmy grabbed Tom by the hand and began leading him down the tunnel.

Tom didn't exactly enjoy situations that made him vulnerable. Putting on a wet, filthy, smelly, blindfold and walking through a cavernous mine with his nine-year-old son and his father's goofy helper leading the way made it tough to look confident.

"Good job, Daddy!"

"Yer a'most thar," Dusty said.

Out of a little gap in the blindfold, Tom saw the ground change from black, to blue, then orange, yellow, purple, and red. His feet were lit up with colors below them, colors that swirled and floated around his work boots. It was beautiful, he had to admit.

"Just a few more steps, Daddy!" Jimmy's voice had that childlike thrill of Christmas morning.

Then they stopped walking, and Dusty untied the blindfold.

Tom was about to tell them what a waste of time this was when the blindfold fell from his eyes and the words caught in his throat.

A crowd of strange little creatures was standing before him.

Chapter 26

There were hundreds of beings—creatures which had somewhat human characteristics, yet distinctly different, all shapes and sizes—standing with their mouths hanging open just as wide as Tom's. Some were bright shades of the rainbow, while others were pastels, neutrals, or fluorescents. Their hair was just as diverse: long, short, spiky, wavy, flowing, and balding. The only thing the creatures had in common, at least from the outside, were their eyes, not in their shape or color—

—but in their kindness.

Tom was in shock, but fear didn't enter the equation. The eyes of the creatures let him know he wasn't in any danger. Still, he was struggling to process everything. Maybe he had fallen and hit his head, and he was unconscious, dreaming about Pappy's Magical Mine Moppets.

There was a moment of awkward silence. In the distance, Tom heard the sound of something like a waterfall. Then he heard one-two-three, and the creatures—what surely must have been Mine Moppets—all burst out into a great, big belly laugh at a pitch so high Tom thought that every dog within miles would descend upon the mine.

He found himself shrinking back from the group. Childhood memories flashed through Tom's mind. How many times had Pappy missed dinner because of the Magical Mine Moppets? At what age had he been old enough to realize that Magical Mine Moppets couldn't possibly exist, that his father simply didn't want to be around him? All that time without his father because of those fictional Magical Mine Moppets.

But they weren't fictional.

Now, all of that had been turned inside out. Pappy was telling the truth!

He looked at the cavern around him. It was a bright and colorful space— the red apples on the trees shimmered, the green stems from the vast varieties of vegetation glistened, and the yellow sun somehow sparkled, though they were hundreds of feet under the ground. Overhead, stalactites hung, with colors like ripples over water. Stalagmites on the ground created a maze, leading to water and trees.

Everywhere, Mine Moppets stuck their heads out of wall crevices, looked at Tom, then dove back into hiding.

"This isn't happening," Tom mumbled.

"Oh, it's happenin'," said Pappy's voice. It sounded like it was coming from the sea of Mine Moppets.

Tom spun around, calling out, "Where are you?"

"Right here," said Pappy, emerging from the Mine Moppets who had surrounded him. He looked somehow taller, more peaceful, and more confident. "Do ya believe me now?"

"No," Tom said in the same tone he had used his entire life when it came to the Mine Moppets. He plopped down right there, sitting in the salt.

Pappy tilted his head. His eyes glanced to the group of Mine Moppets who surrounded him.

Tom hung his head. He knew, common sense right out the window, that he had to admit the truth, and it was magical, this whole place, just as Pappy said. "Yes, Pappy. I believe you."

Tom and Jimmy walked through the cavern in a state of wonder.

This underground colony was alive with hundreds of Mine Moppets of every color, shape, and size. They passed a blue Mine Moppet with orange, curly hair, playing a guitar just outside the grounds of a small house. At his feet was his guitar case, so Tom reached into his pocket, out of habit, and threw in some change. The Mine Moppet smiled and kept playing. As they stepped closer, Tom saw a team of white Mine Moppets, bald and sporting fluorescent yellow jumpsuits, scaling a house built in the walls of the mine to clean the windows. Other Mine Moppets were throwing footballs, enjoying picnics, or reading books on rainbow-colored benches.

As they walked down a path, Pappy shouted out, "I see ya! Don't try ta hide from me!" Suddenly, a young Mine Moppet appeared from behind the nearest tree. He giggled and scampered off, which caused Jimmy to giggle and run after him.

"Jimmy, be careful!" Tom shouted. Jimmy waved back at him and continued chasing the creature through the trees.

"He'll be just fine," Pappy said. "Nothin' bad happens down here."

Tom conceded and followed Pappy along the path that followed a creek. About a hundred feet away, a corn chip canoe powered by an ear of corn gently rolled along, creating subtle ripples in the water. Jimmy returned with a Mine Moppet dog in tow. The dog was bright green, his body shaped like a lime wedge, and he wiggled with excitement. Jimmy joined the group, but the dog jumped into the river, splashing and making a scene.

"Welcome ta Mine Moppet Land," Dusty announced. "It's supper time." He pointed straight ahead, along the creek. "Up thar. That thar tree."

In the distance, Tom spotted a massive tree right in the center of this strange but colorful land. Its leaves were greener, healthier, and more vibrant than any others Tom had ever seen. Tall, straight, and wide, its trunk featured large knots that looked just like soft brown eyes. Its bark was a beauty to behold, like dark brown skin with golden touches.

Then Tom watched its mouth open wide, nearly six feet, into a gentle smile. The tree had a face! The Mine Moppets immediately ran over and began lining up beneath its branches, each taking a bowl and spoon from a stack of crockery and utensils. All except for a lime green, wedge-shaped dog, full of mischief. He bounced up to the front of the line and began jumping and clawing against the tree's trunk.

"That's Spark, the Tree of Inspiration," said Pappy. "And that dog is named Lucky. He's a thorn in everybody's side."

"Lucky don't like ta wait," said Dusty.

"It's just rude," said Pappy. "Cuttin' in line like that. Common courtesy goes a long way, especially at feedin' time."

"Where is dinner?" Tom said.

The tree's enormous mouth slowly began to form words. "Now, now," it said in a deep baritone, "you need to wait in line just as the others do, Lucky. It's not your turn yet."

Lucky wagged his tail, pickup up a bucket in his mouth, then trotted off to the back of the line, the small bucket clenched between his teeth. The Mine Moppets burst into a great big belly laugh.

A bell chimed, a spout on the tree opened up and then a delicious-smelling, thick, reddish-brown liquid began to pour out. Mine Moppets filled their bowls and moved on.

"It's chili!" Tom said. "That tree dispenses chili like a waterfall!"

"Yepper," Pappy said proudly. "That's my chili!"

The Magical Mine Moppets who had stepped up for dinner from the Tree of Inspiration took seats all around and gleefully ate their dinner.

"And it's real chili!" Pappy added. "No beans!"

Tom felt his stomach growl.

Pappy touched his shoulder. "Well, let's move on!"

The group walked on and saw two Mine Moppets in knight's armor, sparring with each other on a small grassy knoll. One tossed a puff of orange powder, which Tom believed to be salt dust, into the other's face and then the other did the same with a puff of blue powder.

138

"Who are those guys?" Jimmy asked, enthralled.

"Those'r the Cumin twins. They're ornery; best ta leave 'em alone."

Suddenly, something swooped over their heads, causing Tom and Jimmy to duck. Tom felt something on his head, and he reached up and found a green, fragrant herb in his hair.

"What in the world was that?"

"That'd be Reggie Bat," Pappy explained. "Such a trickster. But we cain't do without his oregano!"

Just then, a Mine Moppet that resembled a giant clove of garlic wandered aimlessly onto their path. He displayed a sad expression on his face, and when he saw Tom, he stopped.

Pappy nudged Tom. "That's Gary Garlic. He's sort of absent-minded."

The Mine Moppet stopped and looked utterly confused. "Do you know where I can find . . ." he said, lingering on the word find, failing to finish his thought.

"Find what?" Tom asked although he was certain he wouldn't be able to answer. Gary Garlic frowned. "Never mind. I already forgot." Tom caught a whiff of Gary's breath and recoiled.

Gary held up a hand. "I know, I know. You don't have to rub it in."

He waddled off. Pappy said, "Uh-oh. Don't look now." Tom looked around, wondering what could possibly happen that would be stranger than this.

Pappy pointed near a large tree where an oversized purple Mine Moppet stood. "It's Jack Sprat the Brat. He's the one Mine Moppet ya don't want ta cross 'cause he's watched too many movies. He thinks he's the bad guy and likes ta scare people, in jest of course."

Tom had a hard time imagining any of these Magical Mine Moppet creatures being bullies.

They came to a path which led to a drawbridge to another house built into the side of the cavern. This house was grander than the others and sparkled with a rainbow of colors. A crowd was beginning to form nearby, and Pappy took Jimmy by the hand. "I'd like you to meet a very important Mine Moppet. She lives in that thar salt crystal palace you see."

The crowd parted to reveal a beautiful young female Mine Moppet, her outfit a patchwork of a hundred different vibrant colors, a shiny crown atop her humanlike head. Her face resembled that of a rag doll with painted cheeks, mouth, eyes, and nose. It looked as if it was sewn together as there were stitches that ran down the center and upon the sides of her face. She held a rainbow scepter in one hand. In her other hand was a phone which had the characteristics of solid rainbow-colored sparkling stone. Her hair, though, was a tangle of unruly curls.

"Princess Penelope Patch, what have ya done with yer hair?" Pappy asked.

She didn't look up from her phone. "I, like, totally lost my brush. I think someone stole it."

Pappy continued. "Princess Patch, This is my family from upside. This is Tom, my son, and," pointing at Jimmy, "that's Jimmy, my grandson."

She finally looked up at them. Her eyes were a lustrous green. She smiled sweetly, then put her attention back on her cell phone.

"Also, Princess, I've got some bad news," said Pappy, taking off his hat and looking at her with baleful eyes. "It seems as if I could lose ownership of this here mine."

Tom stayed silent. He listened to the conversation, but decided now was not the time to tell Pappy that he had lost his farm to save his beloved mine. He just couldn't bear to tell him he lost the farm. Pappy would be devastated. He needed this mine and its salts, and if Pappy knew he gave up the farm, the one he grew up on, he might never forgive him, and it might ruin his chances of ever recovering his farm. It was the family farm. It had been for generations. So for now, he allowed Pappy to continue to believe he had lost everything.

Pappy explained the situation to the princess, and when he had finished, she looked at him with playful scampishness in her eyes. "This bank president, what's his name?"

"Withers."

"Daddy said that if you bring this Withers down here, we'll make sure that you keep the mine."

She left the method deliciously unstated.

"Thank ya, Princess," Pappy said theatrically.

Princess Penelope Patch turned away and melted away into the crowd of Mine Moppets, still absorbed on her phone.

Jimmy's eyes were nearly popping out of his head. "She's hot!"

Tom put a hand on his shoulder and whispered, "She's a Mine Moppet, son."

Just then, a voice appeared nearby. "Did someone say she's hot! Look at me! I'm the one who's hot! I think I have pneumonia!"

A bright red Mine Moppet, sweating like he'd just come from the gym, wearing ice cubes on a headband around his head, and a strange device strapped to his back, walked toward the group.

"That's the notorious hypochondriac Charlie Chili," said Pappy.

As Charlie drew closer, Tom could see a thermometer sticking out of his mouth.

Charlie Chili was nearly bursting with panic. "Look at me! I'm burning up! Might be the pig flu! That's a killer! You don't know what it's like to be this hot all day and night!"

Jimmy was speechless.

Charlie began to sing. "I want to be a crisp ninety-eight point six. Hey, that's normal. I wanna be cool, build an igloo. Gotta become normal. I'll take an ice cube bath or a brisk long walk in Antarctica.

"Anwherctica?" the Mine Moppets chimed in.

Looking up from her cell phone, Princess Patch asked, "Did he say Antarctica?"

"Yes, Indeedctica!" sang Charlie Chili.

"I think he's lost his mindctica," responded Gary Garlic woefully.

Charlie continued to sing. "Oh, how I'd welcome icicles to cover me, like freezing rain covers trees."

Then he spoke. "Then everyone would see me . . . differently. If I were a nippy 98.6 degrees."

"Wait! doesn't he know he's supposed to be hot?" Jimmy whispered. "He's a chili pepper!"

"It does no good ta tell 'im," Pappy said, shaking his head.

Charlie stumbled off, rambling on about the temperature until he was out of sight.

Jimmy focused his attention back on the princess. "Well I think she's magical, if not hot," Jimmy stated dreamily. He tugged on his grandfather's sleeve. "Where does she live, Pappy?"

"Right thar," he replied, pointing to the palace across the nearby drawbridge. "Do ya want ta go in?"

"Yeah!"

"That's good. King and Queen Patch live here too. But I'm not sure we can enter today."

Jimmy was crestfallen. "Why not?"

"Because that mighty Mine Moppet guard has ta let us in. And he doesn't allow just anybody." Pappy pointed to a palace guard who was positioned in front of the drawbridge. He was a full head taller than Tom and dressed in a stiff, official patchwork uniform. His face was stern, his eyes fixed straight forward.

As they approached him, Tom gulped, but Pappy waltzed right up with no fear. He explained that he'd brought two visitors and introduced Tom and Jimmy.

The palace guard pointed to Jimmy and said, "Hand."

Jimmy looked nervously at Pappy.

"He wants ta see yer hand," Pappy clarified.

Jimmy slowly and nervously held it out to the guard who took it and studied it. Then something strange happened. The guard's chest glowed and became transparent, making his beating heart visible through the patchwork uniform front. With each passing second, it became a warmer shade of red.

"Pure of heart," said the guard. "You may pass."

"That means he'll let ya enter the castle," said Pappy.

Then the second palace guard pointed at Tom's hand. Tom reluctantly lifted it. The guard held his hand, and his chest became transparent and glowed. Then his heart turned a black.

"Not pure," stated the guard. "You may not pass."

Tom looked at Pappy and Jimmy, then turned back to the guard. "Wait! What? I'm pure! I'm a good man. I don't drink. I don't do drugs. I am good and take care of my family. I care about and help others. I am generally nice to most people. Why can't you see? I don't understand."

The guard was silent. He went back to his original stance, his face stern, and eyes fixed straight forward.

"What about the other guard? Maybe this one is broken."

Pappy just shook his head and said, "Nope, nothing is broken here. We can come back another day, son," Pappy continued, solemnly. "People can change."

Tom was dismayed and wondering what Pappy had meant by that as he conceded, and they turned away.

Pappy led the group up a set of stairs to an overlook, where they peered down onto a rainbow salt mining pit.

"This is the Magical Mine Moppet's Kingdom," said Pappy, "and we're fortunate that they let us in now and again. This pit is where salt is mined. Daily tasks have ta be done. I get ta help every now and then. That's how I get my salt ta mix with my chili. But we need ta go now. We have work ta do upside."

"I don't want to leave," said Jimmy.

"I never do," answered Pappy.

Chapter 27

Standing at her son's dresser, Mary Anne suddenly felt the full weight of what she was doing.

The moving boxes lay on the floor, half-filled already. Her husband had come home a few days earlier and announced that they were going to turn over the farm to the bank. Just as simple as that. She couldn't blame him. She turned her head and looked out the window at the thousands of acres of failing Ubercorn. Nobody could figure out the pestilence that was causing this. It was one of the risks that they'd taken by planting a new hybrid. Tom had been a pioneer, rolled the dice, and lost.

She understood all that. It made her sad, extremely sad, to be abandoning this farm, but they had discussed the risks many times. What she didn't understand was the way that he'd gone about it. Tom had come home, as though something sudden had occurred. He didn't want to talk about it, but he said that he'd talked with Withers and that they'd worked out a deal—Pappy would keep his mine if Tom would lose his farm. Tom guaranteed her that there was profit to be made from the mine. He explained that they would be OK, in the long run.

She hoped he was right. She didn't trust Withers and had told Tom that. He'd told her not to worry about it. She did worry, though. First, he had told her his father died, then he was alive. He had told her he miraculously saved himself from a squirrel incident. That wasn't true. She had found that out herself, with Bojangle's help. Now, he had made a deal with the devil.

Mary Anne wiped a tear from her eye. She began putting her son's shirts and shorts into the packing boxes. Children's clothing took up less room than she had imagined.

Then she heard a car arrive and a door slam. She looked out the door. It was Tom.

"Mary Anne!" he shouted.

She stuck her head out the window.

"The hearing is on!"

"What hearing?"

"The one that Withers was supposed to cancel! The mental competency hearing for Pappy! That rat *lied* to me! Pappy called me to remind me! I told him it wasn't happening anymore, but he said it most certainly was!"

Her eyes went wide. Her intuition had been right. It turned out that

Withers couldn't be trusted.

"When is it?"

"In one hour!"

She dropped the clothing and ran out of the room.

The courtroom wasn't adorned with fancy wood or shiny floors, but instead, halogen lights, cheap carpet, and plastic laminate. Tom had thought it would be classier. He and Pappy sat on one side of the room with Pappy's ad litem while Withers, his sharp-dressed state lawyer who looked like his clothing came from a famous designer, and Young Lin sat on the other. The judge wore the typical black robe attire, though he had a youthful face, with hair that needed a good combing, and a yellow and blue Hawaiian colored shirt sticking up beneath his serious black robe.

The judge spoke first. "The court calls the first witness," he adjusted his glasses and held up the docket. "A Mr. Dusty Clements."

Dusty rose from the back of the courtroom sporting his best suit, a haphazard mess of a thing. He smoothed his hair and took the gum from his mouth, placed it in a wrapper and returned it to his pocket.

"Take the stand," the judge instructed.

Dusty looked around, utterly confused.

"That means sit here." The judge nodded toward the chair next to him. Dusty obeyed.

Tom looked at the traitor and wondered how Dusty could have turned on Pappy, who had cared for him all these years. He rested his elbows on the table in front of him. This was going to be a long day.

The state lawyer asked Dusty the usual questions. How long had he worked at the mine? What was his role there? How would he describe the state of the mine?

Then he got to the meat of the questioning. "Have you noticed anything out of the ordinary that would indicate Pappy's memory is starting to fail?"

Dusty looked confused. "Fail? He ain't in school no more."

The state lawyer demonstrated his best level of patience. "I mean, is he starting to lose his faculties?"

Dusty looked as though he were talking to an alien life form. "I already said he ain't in school."

The courtroom let out a moan.

The judge jumped in. "Have you, in your interactions with Pappy, seen

146

any actions or heard anything which would make you believe Pappy is losing his mind?"

Dusty shrugged. "Yeah, sometimes he fergets ta make coffee in the mornin.'"

The observers in the courtroom burst out laughing. The judge angrily banged his gavel. "Order!" he exclaimed.

The people quieted down, and the lawyer stopped skirting around the issue. "Has he ever told you he sees . . . Magical Mine Moppet creatures?"

"Sure," Dusty said. "All the time."

Tom shut his eyes and groaned. He thought back to before he had met the Magical Mine Moppets. If he'd been in the courtroom then, he would have rolled his eyes and said, like he used to, that Pappy was loopy. He wished he could bring one of the Mine Moppets here, to the trial, to show everyone the truth. But that wasn't going to happen.

He knew where this was headed.

It was after lunch when Tom was called to the stand. The state lawyer paced back and forth a few times before launching into his first question.

"There are those who think your father has some unusual ideas about life. Do you believe that is true?" He stopped in front of Tom and tapped the gold ring on his pinky finger against the stand. Tom wondered if this was a tactic to make him feel on edge.

Tom said, "Most people, you could say, have odd ideas about life. I guess you could say he does to an extent. All people believe in things, some real, some not. It is in the eye of the beholder." He could smell the lawyer's cologne, and it reminded him of the stench of hot pine tar. "What I mean is how can you say Mine Moppets *don't* exist?"

The courtroom gasped, but Tom pressed on. "We discover new species of animals all the time, and there aren't enough scientists in the world to catalog all the life out there."

The lawyer smirked. "Living in a cave? Underground?"

"Sure, why not?" Tom remained steady in his speech and demeanor. "That's exactly the type of environment that scientists find new species. We see new places being discovered all the time. There are even places where they have found entire jungles underground. And there are many places deep in the earth that haven't been explored yet, mysteries."

Young Lin leaned forward with his lips pressed tightly together. Tom felt that the man looked concerned, a good sign. Nearby, Withers whispered something into his lackey's ear, and the two of them made hand gestures like they were sitting in the bullpen of a major league baseball game.

"No further questions," said the state lawyer, abruptly.

"You are excused," said the judge.

Tom stood up and left the witness stand. On the way, he caught sight of Young Lin bolting out the back door of the courtroom. "Next witness," said the judge.

Withers and his lawyer were huddled in deep conversation. "We need a few minutes, your honor."

"The court will take a short recess," said the judge, banging his gavel.

Half an hour later, the case resumed. The lawyer stood and said, "We'd like to call a Mr. Lee to the stand."

The courtroom doors flew open, banging both walls, and a man with shoulder-length black hair and a crooked mustache took the stand. Pappy's expression told Tom that the old man had no idea who this new witness was.

"Mr. Lee, you are an expert in biodiversity, correct?" the lawyer asked.

Mr. Lee replied in a tone so ridiculously arrogant that it was hard for Tom not to laugh, though others in the courtroom did just that.

"World renowned, sir."

"Is it possible for a new species of magical creatures to have been living underground, in a cave, undetected by man?"

"It's highly unlikely. Although we have found life under the earth, there has never been a place found through any exploration of any kind of creature outside of those species we are already aware of."

On his feet now, Tom called out, "Your honor, this is absurd. Although we have found millions of species, there are still many unaccounted for or cataloged. He's an imposter. He would know this."

"That's preposterous!" the lawyer exclaimed.

The judge eyed Mr. Lee, then Withers, then the fancy lawyer. He puckered his lips, squinted his eyes, and asked if there were any more questions. Withers looked at his lawyer and dragged his finger across his neck. The imposter was excused, and the judge told the courtroom that he would take another recess and render a decision within the hour.

Tom sat back. There was nothing left to do but allow the judge to decide Pappy's fate.

"This is it, Pappy," said Tom. "What are you thinking?"

The old man seemed pensive. "I'd like some bacon and a pickle."

It seemed a lifetime, but the judge finally returned. He pushed his glasses up on his nose. From somewhere beneath his robe, he produced a children's book and began to read.

"In a hole in the ground there lived a hermit." Everyone in the courtroom looked at one another and then around the room, but the judge didn't seem to notice. He kept reading.

Finally, the judge looked up and said, "It was my favorite when I was young, just a moppet myself. All this talk about Mine Moppets made me want to share it with you." He smiled warmly and then seemed to remember he was in the courtroom.

Tom thought that perhaps the judge was the nutty one here.

The judge slammed the book shut. "As much as I loved this story, I believe that these characters deserve to stay in literature. They don't exist. After reviewing all the reports from prior medical and mental tests performed and the testimonies, I have determined Pappy to be mentally incompetent and unable to care for himself in the ways needed to survive successfully in society. Unless there is anyone who is willing to take responsibility for him and take guardianship, I have no recourse but to have him institutionalized until further notice."

Tom couldn't bring himself to look at his father or anyone else in the room. He stared at the ground, raised his right hand and said, "As his son, I take that responsibility."

"So be it, says I. Hear ye, hear ye. This hearing is over." the judge said and banged his gavel.

Pappy shut his eyes, and Tom squeezed his hand. Across the aisle, Withers stood up, shook his lawyer's hand, grinned, and cackled.

"Thank you, your honor," Withers said. He walked over to Pappy.

"Start packing, Pappy."

Tom leaped forward, about to flatten Withers's nose, but Pappy stepped in, his iron grip on Tom's forearm."

"Don't do it, son," he said. "Not worth it."

Chapter 28

They cleared out the farm, loaded up, and were gone. Tom didn't look back. They drove in silence to the Smegley Motel, just outside town, near the Minute-Mart.

The motel was clean enough, Tom thought, but was it ever grim and depressing. This was the end of the road, he was sure. The farm? Gone. The mine? Gone. His self-respect? Gone forever. The only good out of it all was the fact Pappy had told him the truth. He could finally begin to heal their relationship.

The first night was so difficult—he never thought that his family would be so desperate, that he would be so powerless to help. An air of desperation hung over all of them, including, for once, Pappy. Tom saw his wife crying by herself that evening, and at first, he was going to go to her, comfort her. But he thought it best to let her just get it out. It wasn't as if he had any answers or anything. What could he do? Nothing.

They were homeless and broke, despite all his work and ideas and energy. He was a failure, a loser. He couldn't even show his son that he could fix things. He would never be able to say he was there for him. He wished he would just fall into an open pit somewhere and disappear.

He awoke early the next morning to a pounding on the door. "Who even knows we're here?" he said to a startled Mary Anne.

He stumbled to the door, his back aching from the sagging bed, and opened it to find Madge standing there, dressed in hot pink from head to toe.

"Early to bed, early to rise. They still say that, don't they? Come on, let's get to work!"

He scratched his head absently. "Doing what?"

She folded her arms and looked at him as if he were a complete dunderhead. "I don't know! Something! Let's git on down to the diner and figure it out!"

Tom, Mary Anne, and Jimmy sat crammed into a booth at Madge's Diner. Their faces hung lower than a snake's belly in a wheel rut. They were confused, Tom more than any of them.

On the opposite side of the booth, Pappy had a plate of bacon and a pickle, munching away.

"Pappy, you just lost everything," said Tom. "In twenty-four hours, the mine will legally belong to the bank again."

"Still gotta eat," said Pappy.

"Withers lied to me. He said that he wouldn't submit you to a mental competency hearing."

"People lie," said Pappy, shrugging.

"We lost the farm too," said Mary Anne. "We sacrificed our property to Withers so that you could keep your mine."

"Sorry," he said. They watched as Pappy folded a piece of bacon in half and sliced it lengthwise and wrapped it around a pickle, tying it neatly.

"I think he's in his happy place," said Jimmy.

Upon hearing this, Pappy looked up. "My happy place is with the Magical Mine Moppets. And as soon as we can get Withers down into the mine, they'll take care of everything."

Mary Anne shot a look at Tom, like, What does that mean?

But Tom just shrugged. He had no idea what Pappy or the Mine Moppets had in mind.

Madge ambled over. "OK, what did we figure out?"

"Nothing," Tom said. "Withers and his bunch really creamed us."

"It was the Mighty Bank of Elites," said Madge. "I mean, with a name like that, there's no way they were gonna lose, am I right?"

"You're right," said Mary Anne.

"If there was some way that we could find out that Withers was, in fact, stealing from his bank," said Tom. "If we had concrete proof, we could get out of this."

"I might be able to help. I got some goods, and I think you should act soon. I even came and got your sorry butts out of bed this mornin.'"

Tom stuttered, "We—"

"I know," she interrupted, "but you're slow. Now tell me, who knows everthang what goes on 'round these parts?"

"You do."

"Right!" said Madge. "And I know where you can get proof."

"Where's that?" said Mary Anne.

"In Withers's office."

Pappy suddenly tuned into the conversation. "That's no help. You're gonna have ta be more specific."

"That's gonna cost you," she said.

"What?"

"A piece of strawberry rhubarb pie."

Tom nodded. "We'll take the whole pie if it means getting our farm and his mine back."

"Just a second," she said.

Madge walked away, then returned with a pie and set it down. "I hope you weren't kidding. You just bought yourselves a whole pie."

"I wasn't," he said.

"Good, cause neither was I. You got a pen?"

Tom scrambled for one, then spread out a napkin. "Go."

"So late last night I really grilled that Withers's goon who keeps courtin' me. He says nope, can't tell you nothin'. I say you can, and you will. So, the thing is? He's afraid of spiders. Spiders! So I locked him in the bathroom and started to pour a whole bunch of the little critters under the door. He cries like a teethin' baby and begs to get out, so we made us a deal."

"Awesome!" Jimmy said. "Afraid of spiders! Ha!"

"So whatcha got, Madge?" said Pappy.

"This—Withers keeps all of his off-the-books transactions and dirty stuff separate from the regular books. They're in a top-secret hidey space in the closet where he keeps his assistant."

Tom tilted his head. "He keeps his assistant in a closet?"

"Does that surprise you?"

"Not really, now that you mention it."

Madge shrugged and said, "Now you boys figure it out! I got customers!" And she moved along to the next table.

Tom looked at his father. "We could try to break in."

"We could. How?"

"We could pretend to be plumbers."

Pappy shook his head. "President Nixon did that, that's not me."

"Tom, didn't you say that Withers's office was kind of shabby?" said Mary Anne.

He nodded.

"Well, I don't know. Maybe you could pretend to be painters."

Tom thought about that. "Indeed," he said, "and I think that I know just how to do it."

Chapter 29

Next morning, Pappy and Tom arrived at the service entrance of the bank. They were dressed in new white painter's garb that Jimmy had splattered with paint on the floor.

They wore baseball caps and glasses that they'd bought at the local thrift shop. Tom had dyed his hair jet black. Pappy wore sunglasses and had dyed his beard to hide his very recognizable face.

They pulled behind them a cart full of paint cans.

"Where did you get these?" said Tom.

"Local paint store had 'em."

"Are any of them full? We actually need to paint, at least a little."

"I think the pink un.'"

They entered the service entrance. A rotund supervisor, his sleeves so long they nearly covered his hands, saw them and said, "Main office sent you guys, right?"

"Yep," said Tom. The less said, the better.

"Somebody named Madge called and gave us a heads-up."

"Good woman, that Madge."

"But I thought it would be tomorrow. We didn't clear out the investment banking executives yet," he said. "That was gonna be done tonight."

"They told us that the president's office needed something."

The supervisor looked at them. "I've been trying to get Withers to spruce up his office for years. He won't do it. God knows how much business we've lost because he likes working in an overheated, outdated, and dark dungeon in the sky."

"I think we should give him a surprise," said Pappy.

"So," said Tom, shifting weight, getting ready to put the pressure on, "if we don't paint today, we cancel the contract and go home. It's written right in it. You probably didn't read all the fine print, but it's considered canceled."

"I don't have the wing ready. Like I said, I was gonna do it tonight—"

"What about the president?"

"What about him?"

"Is he in the office today?"

"No, he's out at some farm all morning."

"Let's surprise him." Tom held the man's gaze. "How many years you been here?"

"Twenty-nine."

"He show you any respect in that time?"

"Not once. Come on, follow me."

Dragging their cart of paint cans, Tom and Pappy arrived in Withers's office, the supervisor right behind them. "I don't know, this is kinda dicey—"

"We're color professionals," said Tom.

Pappy spread out a drop cloth and began removing the cans. The supervisor watched him, making no move to leave.

"This is gonna take a while," said Tom. "You can come back in about half an hour."

"All right," he said. The supervisor cleared out and shut the door. Tom immediately ran over and locked the door.

"Pappy, you paint."

"But—"

"We have to play the role, all the way, otherwise we don't get out of here. I'm going to look in the closet."

Pappy shrugged and reached for one of the new paintbrushes. Tom, meanwhile, found the side closet and opened the door. It was a large utility closet, candy wrappers on the floor, a small night light in a corner, a dented file cabinet in the corner. It was a sad excuse for an assistant's office. It showed just how inhuman Withers really was.

He checked every wall but found nothing, and at least fifteen minutes had passed.

"Try the floor," Pappy finally suggested.

Tom peered down. Everything was normal. Then he spotted a corner of the carpet peeling up. That was odd. It seemed to be unanchored to the floor. He bent down and pulled the carpet back. It revealed a safe anchored to the floor, face up.

"Oh great," he said. "What's wrong?" said Pappy.

"It's a safe, and we don't know the combination."

Silence from his father, then: "Can ya just lift the safe?"

Tom thought about it. They could take the whole thing out of the bank, then open it at their leisure. But it probably weighed a ton. He reached down, dug his hands into both sides—and the door of the safe swung open.

"What!" said Tom. "Withers doesn't even lock it."

"He's gettin' sloppy," said Pappy. "Most criminal types do, eventually."

Tom gathered up the papers inside, then closed the safe and covered it with the carpet again. Then he backed out and shut the closet door.

He turned around. His father had painted a huge pink stripe across the entire side of the room.

"Pappy, what's that?"

"I was practicin'. That's the only color we really had."

Tom laughed and painted a stick man on the wall, wrote "Withers" above it, then put the paint cans back on the cart and rolled up the drop cloth. "Let's get out of here!"

Two hours later, in the motel room near the Minute-Mart, Tom and Pappy and Mary Anne sat down, studying the papers.

"Holy cow," said Mary Anne, scanning the document. "Look at the P & Ls on this one. It doesn't even come close to matching what's on his tax return."

"This one is even worse," said Tom. "He's been getting inside loans and siphoning a few thousand dollars a month from the mortgage department."

"The same department that is taking back our properties."

"Exactly."

Mary Anne turned to Pappy. "What about you, Pappy? What have you found?"

"A few old bearer bonds," said Pappy. "And a receipt for hair plugs."

Chapter 30

Jimmy stepped out of the Minute-Mart, a bottle of vanilla cream soda in his sticky fist. A black SUV was parked nearby, its engine running. One of the windows rolled down. Inside were two of Withers's goons.

"Hey Jimmy," one said.

He ignored them. He remembered them from when they had visited the farm with Withers, and he didn't like them at all.

"Jimmy, the Mine Moppets have a message for you."

That caught his attention. He turned and approached the car. "You know the Magical Mine *Moppets*?"

"Sure," said the goon. "We work for Pappy sometimes. Pappy and Mr. Withers are old friends. They go way back. Anyway, the Mine Moppets gave us a message for you. They want us to bring you back to the mine to hang out."

Jimmy's fingers tightened around the bottle of soda so tightly that he thought he would break the glass. "That would be awesome!" he said. "I do want to talk to the king and queen about something."

"You want to leave right now?" said one.

"No," said Jimmy, "I have to buy something for Princess Penelope Patch first."

The goon looked tickled at that. "Really? She must be very beautiful."

"Oh, she is, she's the most beautiful creature I ever saw. But I need to find some more money first."

The goon held out a ten-dollar bill. "This enough?"

Ten bucks! Jimmy thought.

"Here, just pay me back when you can."

"Thanks! Where do you want me to meet you?"

"Right here," said the goon. "We'll be waiting for you."

"I can't ride with strangers," Jimmy said.

"What *strangers*? You've seen us plenty!"

Jimmy had. "OK, be right back. This is gonna be cool!" Jimmy took a swig of the soda pop, then chucked it into the trash and ran for the store, eager to buy a new hairbrush for Princess Patch.

Mary Anne was still sitting at the table in the motel, poring over the family finances, when the phone rang. She picked up on the second ring.

"Hello? Yes."

As she listened, she felt like a shock of electricity had hit her. "That's odd. No, I don't know where he is. He left earlier to walk to the park. He never misses practice, especially not on Wednesday afternoons." She listened further, not believing what she heard. "I'm gonna have to get back to you."

Mary Anne disconnected and shot to her feet. She ran across the room and reached for her coat. "Jimmy, please don't tell me you went off exploring again."

Just as she closed the motel room door, she heard the phone ring again. She fumbled for her keycard and opened it up and ran over.

Breathlessly, she said, "Hello?"

It was a familiar reedy voice—Withers. "Mary Anne," he said, "I'm glad I caught you. This afternoon, I found somebody, and you better cooperate if you want the little twerp back again! Hey, Jimmy. Say hello to your mother."

Mary Anne heard a voice in the background shout, "Mommy!"

It was Jimmy. Withers had kidnapped him.

"You had better not lay a *hand* on my son, or you will feel the wrath of this mother buffalo stampeding all over your face!" Mary Anne didn't even know what she was saying, or if it even made sense. She didn't care. She felt pure rage against this man threatening to keep her child.

"I got an anonymous phone call about some alleged proof of my wrongdoing," he continued. "Apparently it hints that I've engaged in some, well, questionable activities at the bank. That's ludicrous, but just to be sure, why don't you talk to that anonymous caller, and have him bring those documents to Pappy's mine. And let him know that he'd better do it now—before I sell this brat to pirates."

The line disconnected. Mary Anne stood there, staring at the receiver, feeling her world start to fall apart. Then she screamed, "Tom, where are you!"

At the Powers farm, Tom stood at the edge of the field, studying the gray stalks. He was making his final goodbye. He had to see it one more time, though he wouldn't come back here, not again. It was too painful.

He nudged a rock with the toe of his shoe. Then he picked it up and threw it as hard as he could into the field of gray, dead Ubercorn stalks. It landed with a distant thud as his phone rang.

The rock landed against a tiny, green, live stalk of Ubercorn. At its base, Lacey, the Skeletonizer Beetle, watched as the rock nearly hit her. She sat stunned, trying to determine how a rock suddenly dropped from the sky. It seemed to her that, lately, all kinds of strange things were dropping down from nowhere. But eager to return to her task, she lifted up and inched toward a package of Pappy's Chilly Mountain Chili Mix. She then dragged it to her small pile of mix, opened it, unceremoniously poured it onto the pile, and scooped part of the contents into her tiny patchwork canvas bag. She started her process again and watched as dozens and dozens of Withers's worms and beetles ran for the hills.

Chapter 31

Tom, Mary Anne, and Pappy tore across the desert scrubland, ignoring the sign that welcomed them to *Pappy's* Chilly Mountain Salt Mine.

None of them said a word. Their faces were drawn tighter than a drumhead. Tom's hands squeezed the steering wheel, and his mouth was harder than a bullet. Mary Anne had turned gray and picked at her cuticles. Pappy said nothing in the backseat.

There were two black SUVs at the entrance to the mine. Tom parked next to them and burst out of the car angrily. Nobody was visible.

Pappy opened the door to the office. Dusty sat there, the television blaring, drawing a picture of his dream vehicle. Seeing Pappy, he fumbled to put the drawing away.

"You!" said Pappy.

"I'm here," he said, rather guiltily.

"We don't care," said Tom, arriving behind Pappy. "How many are there?"

"Four," he said, then he lowered his voice. "Plus the boy."

"You didn't do anything to stop them!" screamed Mary Anne. "What kind of human *are* you!" She started at him, but Tom held her back.

"He wanted to see the Mine Moppets!" explained Dusty. "They're not hurtin' 'im!"

Tom realized that Dusty was too simple to get what had really happened.

Dusty said, "Sorry, Pappy. I kinda panicked."

Pappy nodded, knowingly. "I know, Dusty."

Ten minutes later, they were running through the mine tunnels, shouting for Jimmy. Tom tripped but recovered his footing before falling down. Mary Anne wasn't so lucky—she went sprawling on the floor of the tunnel, injuring her knee.

"Keep going!" she said. "I'll be all right. Find our boy!"

Tom kissed her on the head. "I'll be back!"

"I think they might've wandered down the pink wing," said Pappy. "I can smell somethin' differ'nt in the air."

"Then let's go." But Pappy seemed hesitant. "What's the matter?"

"It's not stable down there. Pink salt collapses the easiest. I rarely go there."

Tom thought about it. "Well, then we'll tread lightly."

Pappy led them down a corridor that opened up to the left. Tom found himself creeping through a zig-zagged tunnel lined with translucent pink salt.

"This is going to take forever," Tom stated. "We are going way too slow. We have to find Jimmy. Are you sure they would have gone down this path? If they didn't know it was dangerous, they would have gone faster, don't you think? Then we would have already faced disaster. Maybe we should go back and try another path. I don't see or hear anything."

"No, I tell ya, the nose knows. I fer sure smell it differ'nt now. We gotta keep goin'," Pappy responded.

Tom agreed, and they continued on.

"Jimmy!" he shouted. "Where are you?"

"Daddy!" came a distant voice.

Tom started to run, dodging left, dodging right, without caring about the danger. He had to find his son. The tunnel grew lower, and the occasional dangling light bulb became less and less frequent, making seeing more and more difficult as he went on.

At last, he turned a corner and saw two goons and his son in a little sort of room, which had been carved into the mine walls, dimly lit by the light of a single lantern in one of their hands. Withers was next to them, Young Lin close behind. Jimmy had been shackled to the wall with a leg iron on one of his ankles.

"Give me the documents," Withers said. "No need to panic."

"Let him go!"

Withers spat the next words. "Documents *first*."

Tom reached into his pocket, removed the sheaf of papers, and laid them on the ground halfway between them. With one eye trained cautiously on Tom and Pappy, Withers reached forward and picked them up. Then he looked through them and, satisfied, stuffed them in his inner coat pocket.

"Now give me my son," said Tom.

"Absolutely. But stay put."

Withers nodded to his goons, and one grabbed a sledgehammer and began pounding at the side of the bolt that held Jimmy's leg iron to the wall.

"Sorry about all the theatrics," Withers said, "But I couldn't let you just—"

Withers's sniveling was interrupted by a deep rumbling from above. The ceiling between them began to shudder and groan. Tom and Pappy leaped backward. Suddenly, with the sound of a thunderclap, the roof caved in. The whole earth shook a moment more. Tom and Pappy coughed and nearly choked as the clouds of dust engulfed them.

When the movement had stopped, and the dust settled, there was an enormous pink wall of rock salt and boulders between themselves and Withers's gang. And Jimmy. Darkness surrounded them, except for a small sparkle of light from the pink salt.

After gaining control of his breathing, Tom leaped to his feet and began shouting his son's name. To his surprise, he heard Jimmy's raspy voice reply, "I'm here." He sounded small and far away.

"Are you hurt?"

"No, Daddy, but I can't get out. And it's dark. I'm scared."

"I'm going to get help."

"Hurry!" said Jimmy.

Pappy caught Tom's arm. "The Mine Moppets will know how to take care of this, and we don't have much time before they run out of air."

"Let's hurry then," said Tom.

His father caught his arm a second time. "Only King Patch and Queen Patch have the authority to lead a dig of this kind, especially here. The Magical Mine Moppets don't venture far from home."

Tom was confused. "What does that mean?"

"Means they have ta be consulted first."

"We don't have time for consulting."

"We do if we want ta have help from the Magical Mine Moppets. What we don't have time for is outside help ta get here."

"I hope you're right. Let's go."

"Why don't ya stay here? They're in the castle, and ya have to be pure of heart ta cross the bridge."

"I don't care about protocol. What I do care about is getting my son out of here. They have to let me in."

"They don't even know ya, but they do know me. I'm his grandpa. It will be better if I go in. And faster."

"Well, he's my son. I will not let anybody take my place again."

"OK, but we'd better hurry," Pappy answered.

They proceeded out of the pink salt wing and back into the main corridor where Dusty had picked up Mary Ann.

Tom called out to Dusty as he passed by. "Take care of her. I have to save Jimmy."

Moments later, he and Pappy arrived at the wooden door. Pappy gave his special knock. Soon a Mine Moppet showed up, and Tom burst through the door. The last time, he had not seen the way. He was lost now, so Pappy guided him through the rainbow tunnel. He led him toward a waiting chain of mine carts. Tom reached out to touch one of the carts, half expecting it to disappear from his imagination the moment his finger made contact. But it didn't. The cart was as real as his own toes. It was shaped like a chili pepper, and when he drew his finger back, something sparkly came with it. He rubbed his forefinger against his thumb, and a rainbow ash fell to the ground. He knew, unmistakably, the cart was made of the rainbow salt.

Pappy hopped in the front car. "Let's hurry up, son. It's not good ta keep the king and queen waiting, and there's not much air left in that room." Tom wiped the sweat from his brow. He was not ready to get in one of these cars. It did not look safe at all.

Suddenly, a Mine Moppet shoved him from behind, and Tom tumbled into the second mine cart. The Mine Moppets giggled and pushed his legs all the way in.

"You OK?" said Pappy.

"No! I am not OK! I am in a cart made of salt! Remember what just happened?"

"It's OK," Pappy responded. "This is the strongest salt."

Just then, several of the Mine Moppets placed their hands on the carts and began to push. They picked up speed quickly, since the salt was light, and soon his head was whipping backward with the movement of the chili pepper cart.

Tom screamed like a school girl as the mine cart zipped through the cavern. He stayed crouched down, his eyes peeking over the rim, glimpsing rainbow stalagmites, stalactites, and fingers of rock.

Pappy, on the other hand, kicked his feet up in the front cart and folded his hands behind his head, calm and collected. Now and again, he swiped a lazy finger alongside the blurry walls.

"My first time down here," he yelled back, "hoo boy, I didn't think I would make it!"

At last, the zigging and zagging, the dips and twists, came to an end. The mine cart stopped at a wall. Struggling to catch his breath, Tom wobbled his way out of the cart and onto his two feet. He looked at the wall. There were no bright colors and no traces of salt, only stone.

"Then I realized," said Pappy, "that it was only going about ten miles an hour."

He still had the same smile on his face, which was a good sign. He threw his arms out to the side and yelled, "Pappy has arrived!" Immediately, the decrepit rock wall parted in two, and then those sections split in two again. Everything around Tom moved, and the ground shook like an earthquake shifting the world before his eyes. The pieces of wall lowered into slats that opened up in the ground, making them disappear altogether, and revealing an incredible land, more extravagant than anything Tom had ever seen, even than what he had seen on his last visit. This place was incredible, he thought. He thought there was no wonder why Pappy didn't want to leave. He blinked multiple times, wondering if he were hallucinating.

"Pappy?" Tom asked. "Do you see what I see?"

"Yes, and it never gets old, son."

Before them, in the near distance, was a massive castle for the rulers of the Magical Mine Moppets.

Tom marveled at the castle, complete with turrets, balconies, a moat, and a drawbridge, all made with rainbow salt. Under his feet was a road that looped and curved, leading them to the castle entrance. But he knew he had no time to gawk: Jimmy was in danger, and time was running out. He ran down the long road to the castle, through the land of the Mine Moppets, dodging the oregano bat, avoiding Gary Garlic, and generally trying to keep himself from panicking.

The guard at the castle drawbridge loomed ahead, and Tom slowed himself down.

Pappy caught up to him a moment later.

Tom took a deep breath and announced to this new guard, "I came here before, but to the palace. The guard there would not let me through. But I must get through. My son is in danger, and the king and queen have to help me. I've changed my ways. I love my son. I made peace with this man, my father."

But the guard's chest didn't change color. The guard shook his head at Tom.

Tom reached deeper within himself. He knew he must get through. This had to work. He was not about to let anyone take his place as a father ever again.

He gazed at Pappy, his father, the one who had spent so much time away. He was not perfect, as he had been absent from his family many times, but he realized Pappy was a good, hard-working man. He had thought he was doing all he did so he could take care of his family, which he had done, he had just become caught up in a new life without thinking of the effects it had caused, being an absent father. But one thing was for certain, Pappy had not been lying about the Magical Mine Moppets, after all.

Now, through these last few weeks, Tom had realized that he, himself, had made the same kind of mistakes, only differently. He had to make things right. He tried once more.

"I'll never lie to Mary Anne again. She means the world to me. I'm going to spend more time with my boy. Not because I have to, but because I want to. I commit to being the father I should have been all along. Just please remember that—I am making my family whole again."

The guard didn't move. Tom felt the words pour out. "Pappy, he's a good man after all. I never believed because I was selfish. I wanted Pappy home. I didn't realize he did everything for his family. I was young. I couldn't understand that. Maybe he could have spent more time with us, but we didn't believe. He tried to show me, but all I saw was a crazy man. I saw the worst in him, not the best. I didn't think he loved me. He's not perfect, I know that. But we all make mistakes. I've learned from Pappy's mistakes and my own. I forgive, and I am forgiven. I love, and I am loved. I know how important love is, I know how caught up in material things I was. I want to rebuild trust, begin anew, leave the past where it belongs. I want to truly live."

He closed his eyes, took a deep breath, and exhaled. He began to react as all the anger and hardness began to melt away and then as an overwhelming sense of love and forgiveness overtook him. His face softened. He was wrong about how he treated Pappy, Mary Ann, and Jimmy. He now saw the world with gratitude. He felt whole.

When he opened his eyes, the guard's chest was still dark, and Tom started to cry. This was his last hope. Then, slowly, the heart on the guard's chest lightened, brightened, from gray, to tan, then orange— then bright red.

Tom had passed.

For the first time in years, Tom and Pappy truly embraced. Then Tom walked past the guard. Pappy started to follow, but the guard put his arm out, blocking him. Pappy laughed and playfully pushed the Mine Moppet guard's arm aside and continued on.

The two men hurried across the bridge. They passed the curtain wall and through the gatehouse into the inner court. From there, they entered a massive ballroom that echoed with every step. They rushed to the colorful dais at the far end of the hall, where in their ornate thrones, sat King and Queen Patch, leaders of the Magical Mine Moppets. Their skin resembled the most beautiful of patchwork quilts, and each of them held rainbow salt scepters. Their hands featured only three fingers and a thumb.

Pappy walked forward and bowed with a flourish. The king gestured slowly, like a rock sculpture coming to life, waiting for Pappy to speak.

"Sorry ta ignore protocol, Kingie, but there's an emergency." He quickly described the situation regarding Withers, the blackmail, the goons, Jimmy, and the caved-in ceiling in the pink corridor.

King Patch's brow furrowed, and he rose from his throne. "Mine Moppets! There has been a cave-in. Emergency crews! To your stations! We have very little time. By my calculations, and experiences with cave-ins, we have less than one hour to free little Jimmy."

"And I," the queen announced, "know how to handle this Withers fellow."

King Patch led the way, with Queen Patch, Pappy, and Tom following right behind. He led them through the Mine Moppet kingdom, taking a different way back to the pink wing.

The minutes counted down, too slowly for Tom, although they were nearly running. He hoped this was a short-cut. It had taken nearly three-fourths of an hour to get to the castle, so his anxiety was heightened. His thoughts raced with him as he ran knowing it was essential they made it there in time.

Half an hour later, Pappy and Tom arrived at the site of the cave-in. Behind them was an army of nearly fifty Mine Moppets, all armed with shovels, spades, and other tools of excavation.

Tom shouted, "Jimmy! Are you there?"

"I'm here, Daddy!" came Jimmy's muffled reply.

Queen Patch approached the pile of pink salt. She yelled out, "Withers! Is there a man named Withers in there!"

"Yes," said a weak voice from the other side.

"My name is Queen Patch. I have fifty volunteers willing to dig you out, but I need something from you first."

"What?" "You must promise to serve me as a court jester for the next year. And give up all legal rights to this mine. Return them back to Pappy."

"And Tom's farm," said Pappy.

"Oh, yes! And Pappy's son's farm!"

"I don't know who you even are. Forget it!" Withers weakly shouted back. "I still have Jimmy!"

"Fine!" the queen said, "then we will dig out Jimmy and seal you and your henchmen back in there again! We are hundreds-to-one of you! We are the Magical Mine Moppets!"

"They don't exist. This is all a hoax!"

"Have it your way," the queen replied. "Start digging boys, and make sure it's Jimmy who gets out."

"Sure thing, your majesty," one of them replied. "We know exactly where he is."

"Wait!" There was a long pause. "All right, I give up," the voice replied.

She turned to the Mine Moppets and nodded. They leaped forward and began shoveling the pink salt at an unbelievable rate without disturbing the fragile pink salt walls around them. Tom stood back, watching in amazement as clouds of pink salt whizzed by his head until Jimmy's head burst up through the pink salt, the boy sputtering and shaking salt from his hair.

"Jimmy!" he shouted.

"Daddy!"

He ran forward and pulled his son out and held him close. "I'm here for you, son. From now on, I'll always be. I was wrong. I put other things, things I thought in my crazy mind were more important than the relationship I had with you and your mom, first. I'm sorry I lied to you about Pappy. I never should have done that. I was embarrassed by him, this crazy man, whom I didn't think loved me. I was wrong on all of that. I am going to make 'all' right. I told the guards at the castle, and now, I promise you." He looked around at Pappy. "That means you too, Dad. Hear ye, hear ye, I do so declare! Please, I ask your forgiveness."

Jimmy looked up at his daddy and began to cry tears of joy. "That's all I wanted. I forgive you, Daddy."

Pappy threw his arms around Tom. "Tommy, from now on, I will always be there for you. And Jimmy, too. I promise."

All three generations of Powers men held each other.

Then a group of Mine Moppets came bearing Mary Anne in their arms. She had watched quietly as she had witnessed Tom finally making things right.

"Oh, thank God you are all right!" she said breathlessly.

Tom heard her and turned and reached out to her. Hugging her, Tom said, "From now on, I'll be there whenever Jimmy needs me. And I promise I'll never lie to either of you again."

Next to them, Withers was being plucked out of the pile of salt by an enormous, frowning Mine Moppet. He looked around angrily. "Don't you buffoons realize what you've got here? This salt is invaluable! It's going to make billions!"

"It's just salt," said Tom.

"For chili," added Pappy.

"No," screamed Withers, "you dolts! It's rainbow salt! It's worth two thousand an ounce. More than *gold.*

"And that's why you're going to sign it all back over to Pappy," said Queen Patch, tickling beneath his chin with an index finger, "or else you're never getting out of here."

Withers looked at her, wild-eyed—then began screaming again. "What are you! Leave me alone! I want that salt! Boys, Young Lin, get them!"

The Mine Moppets grabbed him and finally dragged him from the corridor and spirited him deep into their lair until his echoes of protest finally faded into silence.

Suddenly, Jimmy broke the silence. "Wait! What about the goons? I know what they did. They killed your corn, Daddy! That was what I kept trying to tell you. Withers had them do it. They planted mean worms and beetles created just to destroy it. I saw them go in there the day the investors came out when I took Lacey back in the fields. She saw it too. My friend, Lacey, has been working nonstop to fix it."

"That is very good news, Jimmy," said Queen Patch. "We know just the thing to take care of these earth haters." She commanded another group of Mine Moppets to take the goons away.

Princess Penelope Patch arrived, as usual, always just missing the action, her hair even more disheveled than before. She was texting and barely looked at anybody. "What did I miss?"

Jimmy, seeing her, dropped his mouth and stared with starry eyes at the princess, all while tugging at the king's white ermine cloak.

She looked at him and asked, "Does he always look like that? Is he made that way?"

The crowd laughed, and Jimmy popped out of his trance. He looked up at the king, motioned to something in his hand, and pointed to the princess.

King Patch cleared his throat. "Dear, nice for you to grace our presence. Little Jimmy has something for you."

Sheepishly, Jimmy took a few steps forward and presented her with the crinkled bag from the thrift store. "It's a gift," he said nervously.

She finally looked up from her phone, took the bag, and rummaged inside. "Are you kidding me?" she asked, shock on her face.

"I didn't know if that was the right one, but I tried."

She stared at Jimmy. "There's nothing in there but a plain old rock!"

Jimmy frantically looked inside, only to pull out a chunk of rock. "Somebody must've swiped it! It was your clam-shaped rainbow-colored brush!"

Just then another head poked up out of the salt. It was Withers's assistant,

Young Lin. He held up a rainbow-colored clam brush. "Does this look familiar?" he said conspiratorially.

Princess Patch screamed in delight and ran over to this handsome stranger. She threw her arms around him and said, "I don't know who you are, but I feel so connected to you right now."

Young Lin smiled and looked around at the others. "My lucky day!"

Tom put an arm around Jimmy. "The princess is too old for you anyway, son. There will be others."

Mary Anne agreed and kissed Jimmy on the cheek, who promptly wiped it off.

"I love you," she told him.

"How about me?" Tom said.

His wife kissed him on the lips. "I love you and forgive you. Let's go back to the surface."

"Not yet," said Pappy. "There's one more place I want to show you."

Twenty minutes later, the group strolled through a pair of swinging doors into the Mine Moppets' saloon.

A celebration was in full swing. Mine Moppets of all different varieties were laughing, leaping, jumping, and singing.

Some were quaffing tall glasses of liquid.

"What are they drinking, Daddy?" said Jimmy.

"That's salt brine," said Pappy. "It's pretty stout. Ya wouldn't like it. Everybody stick together now. It can get rowdy in here."

They moved through the crowd. One Mine Moppet jostled Pappy, and he pushed him off playfully. Others threw their arms around Tom, Mary Anne, and Jimmy, jabbering in a tongue that nobody understood.

They found a place at the bar. Pappy ordered a round of green salt brines, and when they came, Tom looked at it with trepidation.

"Oh, just throw it back," said Pappy. "It won't hurt ya. Maybe make ya feel a little parched, that's all."

Tom lifted the glass to his mouth and threw it back. It carried salty, sweet, and sour overtones. But mostly, it was just salty.

There was a stage at the other end of the bar. A Mine Moppet shaped like a slab of salt was warbling into a microphone while a country band plucked their old-timey instruments behind her. On the stage next to her were a team of two dancers, also shaped like salt slabs, in can-can dresses doing old-timey jigs, reels, and other country moves.

"Dancing salt," noted Tom. "What next?"

"That would be the Shaker Sisters. One beauty sings, and the others dance. And watch out for the Peppercorn square dancers. Sometimes they get a little carried away."

A pair of square dancers spun out of control and flew into a table, knocking over several glasses of blue, green, and red salt brines.

"Dad, I'm sorry I ever doubted you," said Tom.

He clapped his son on the back. "I'm sorry too. For everything. But we're together now."

They clinked brines.

"It's been really fun, Pappy, but we should go back upside. It's getting late. Jimmy's nodding over there," Mary Anne noted. "And I need to go take care of this knee."

"All right," Pappy answered.

They walked out together, Pappy carrying Jimmy and Tom with his arm around Mary Anne supporting her. Their day was expended and long.

Charlie Chili suddenly appeared. He stopped them midstream. "Wait! Did you say all right? I'm always asking Reggie Bat if I look all right. Feel my forehead. It's burning hot! I've got to go find a place to cool off, and quickly! Anyone got an ice cube? My Ice Cubinator's broken."

Jimmy groggily lifted his head and asked, "What's an Ice Cubinator?"

"It's what makes the ice cubes for my head," replied Charlie Chili, pointing to his hip. "I have it right here for ready use. Since it's broken, maybe if I go with you I can cool off. A hundred and seven degrees is just plain miserable. Is it winter up there?"

Pappy answered matter-of-factly, "Not this time, Charlie. King Patch would not approve. Anyway, it's not winter."

"You just let me know when it's winter. I'll be there."

"We'll see."

They walked away as Charlie looked on forlornly. Charlie took his thermometer and put it in his mouth.

Chapter 32

One month later . . .

Beneath the radiant, mighty, rainbow stalks of Ubercorn, the Powers hosted a community picnic. A sign read *Welcome Back Ubercorn.*

Tom moved through the crowd, greeting people, making tabulations.

A neighbor greeted him, saying, "It's good to see this farm back, Tom. When do you think Ubercorn will be ready?"

"We harvested our first crop last week, and it fetched twenty-two percent more per pound than we'd thought. It's a great start."

Tom moved onto the next person, Leon Redgatingtonson, from down the highway. "So it's official?" Leon asked. "The farm is all yours again?"

"Absolutely," he said, producing the title from his pocket. "Signed, sealed, and delivered, it's mine. I was able to secure my investors with the revival of my crop."

Nearby, Tubby dozed in a chair, a half-eaten ear of corn dangled from one hand. Tom kicked the sole of Tubby's shoes. Tubby jerked awake, then immediately went back to eating his corn. "Hey boss, what is it? You want to go up in the plane or something?"

"No, Tubby, I was just thinking about how that Skeletonizer Beetle has saved us a fortune. Without her, we never would've found out that Withers was killing the plants with worms."

Tubby grew introspective. "It's funny how the worm turns."

Tom turned and stared out at the horizon. There was nothing but pure Ubercorn, healthy and strong, as far as he could see. "I never thought that three thousand and one packets of my dad's chili mix would ever come in handy."

At the base of an Ubercorn plant, Lacey the Skeletonizer Beetle sprinkled the last of a packet of Chili Mix around the crops. She pulled out a pad and paper, flipped past a page that read 12 worms left, *and then she wrote:* Worms left on the farm – Zero!

Jimmy was running through the cornfields, on his way to the picnic, looking for Lacey. He saw her and ran excitedly to where she had finalized her task. Bending down, he scooped her up in his palm. He saw a little notebook in her tiny hands. He couldn't read it, but it sure did look like scribbling of some sort.

He took off again, running like the wind through the cornfield and exited right where he needed to be.

Jimmy ran up to his daddy, holding Lacey in the palm of his hand. "Daddy, I have Lacey here!"

Tom leaned in and peered at Lacey. "Lacey the Skeletonizer Beetle, you are the real hero here!"

The little creature whipped off its gas mask and saluted Tom.

"Hey, Daddy!" Jimmy exclaimed excitedly. "When I went to visit the Mine Moppets with Grandpa Pappy last week, King and Queen Patch said they know Lacey and can talk to her and she can talk to them. And I think she can write too. See her little book. I can't read it, but it looks like words. Can we bring her to the mine later?"

"Of course!"

His son grinned and ran off.

Madge appeared out of the crowd and sidled up alongside Tom. "You'll never guess who my new boyfriend is."

"Oh, I think I can."

Pappy ambled up and took the crook of Madge's arm. "She says she loves me, and we're gonna be married."

"Looks like free bacon and pie for life," said Tom.

"Absolutely," said Pappy. "All with a side of juicy gossip, and pickles."

Just then a familiar black sedan roared up the driveway. Instead of one of the usual bank goons stepping out, it was Dusty who emerged from the back. He handed Pappy the deed and said, "S'all yers Pappy. As of three today, ya got yer mine back. I fixed it fer ya." Tears glistened in the old man's eyes. Tom hugged him.

Dusty continued. "Was easy. Withers ain't thar.. It's been two months and no one seen ner heard a peep from 'im since. They figured he done gone off the deep end an' run away. I didn't tell 'em nuttin'. I just give 'em them papers he give you'ze and they was processed right away." He paused momentarily then asked, "Watcha want me ta do next, boss?"

Tom gestured to the trash all around the party. "If you want to really help," he jokingly commanded, "clean up this mess—and don't complain about it."

Dusty hung his head, back in real life again. He picked up a broom and swept a pile of chili packages into the trash. He conceded that this was the least he could do considering all the trouble he had helped put his dear Pappy through.

He was sincerely sorry for his actions and had expressed this to Pappy. He had asked Pappy to forgive him. Pappy, the kind, loving man that he was, had forgiven him unconditionally. That meant the world to him. He vowed to never let his own selfish thoughts take over to hurt someone else. He felt peace.

Meanwhile, in Mine Moppet Land . . .

Deep underground, Withers was tied with super-strong yellow licorice rope to a rainbow-hued rock.

He giggled hysterically as he was tickled. So did the entire Royal Court, who enjoyed the happy sound of laughter as Young Lin served them a very salty dinner.

"Wait! Tickler!" The king held up his hand, "A little lower, right under the ribcage. There! How's that feel, Withers? You like that? We love to see others become happy."

"Make them stop. Make them stop!" Withers laughed, then scowled, "Please!"

Charlie Chili walked by and noticed Withers's red face. "Mister, looks like you got a fever just like me! Let's see." He whipped out the thermometer from his mouth and crammed it into Wither's mouth.

Withers spit out the thermometer. He sputtered and spit, attempting to remove the burning sensation from his mouth and shouted, "That's as spicy as—"

"Oh no, you got it bad," Charlie interrupted. "I better cool you down quick." He went to his special 'Ice Cubinator'. Charlie pulled out an extra ice headband from his belt. He removed ice cubes from his Ice Cubinator, placed them in ice cube holders of the headband, and placed it in the center of Withers's forehead and around the back of his head.

Withers screamed in shock. "Stop him! This chili creature is piping mad!"

"Wrong! I'm piping hot, and so are you."

"Young Lin! Save me! I'm going insane!" Withers yelled.

"Should I?" Young Lin asked Princess Penelope Patch.

She thought a moment, then said, "I don't know! Should you?"

Young Lin thought about it a moment, then said, "Nah!" and refilled the king's glass with a special brine blend.

Tickler continued his special touch on this extremely difficult character to tame.

Withers's laughter echoed throughout Magical Mine Moppet Land.

CPSIA information can be obtained
at www.ICGtesting.com
Printed in the USA
LVOW08s0000010817
543351LV00008B/137/P